TURN THE PAGE

By Ditter Kellen

www.ditterkellen.com

Copyright © by Ditter Kellen

All rights reserved. This copy is intended for the original purchaser of this e-book ONLY. No part of this e-book may be reproduced, scanned, or distributed in any printed or electronic form without prior written permission from Ditter Kellen. Please do not participate in or encourage piracy of copyrighted materials in violation of the author's rights. Purchase only authorized editions.

Image/art disclaimer: Licensed material is being used for illustrative purposes only. Any person depicted in the licensed material is a model.

Published in the United States of America

This e-book is a work of fiction. While reference might be made to actual historical events or existing locations, the names, characters, places and incidents are either the product of the author's imagination or are used fictitiously, and any resemblance to actual persons, living or dead, business establishments, events, or locales are entirely coincidental.

Warning

Ditter Kellen

This e-book contains sexually explicit scenes and adult language and may be considered offensive to some readers. This e-book is for sale to adults ONLY as defined by the laws of the country in which you made your purchase. Please store your files wisely where they cannot be accessed by under-aged readers

Dedication

For Cathe Green, one of the most beautiful women I have ever known. The impact she has had on my life is astounding and I will always hold a place for her inside my heart.

Here's to her happily ever after.

Chapter One

Catherine Grier buttoned her coat and slipped on a pair of worn green gloves she'd gotten for Christmas some years back. The forecast was calling for sleet this morning, and she had a six-block walk to work ahead of her. She dreaded the cold almost as much as she dreaded her birthday.

An image of her college sweetheart's laughing face floated through her mind. *"Come on, Cathe. It's your birthday...it'll be fun. I'll be careful."* If only she'd said no and insisted they wait for the storm to pass before climbing on the back of his motorcycle, maybe he'd still be alive...as would their unborn child.

Craig and Cathe had been inseparable as only first loves could be, and not a day went by that she didn't miss him. The unplanned pregnancy had been a shock, but they'd been determined to keep the baby and had even begun picking out names.

A wave of sorrow passed through her with the memory of waking in intensive care only to realize that Craig was gone and she no longer carried their child. Cathe hadn't celebrated her birthday since their deaths on that very day, twenty-seven years ago.

Forcing her thoughts aside, she checked her appearance in the mirror on her way to the door. At forty-seven years old, she was still very attractive. Her blonde hair hung in layers to her shoulders, and aside from a few small laugh lines, her face was devoid of wrinkles. She'd managed to keep her girlish figure and received compliments daily on her striking blue eyes.

The icy wind stung her cheeks as she made her way outside, dipping her chin deeper into the pale green scarf wrapped around her neck. Puffs of smoke escaped her mouth with every breath she took, only to be swept away on the frigid February wind.

With a slight wave of her hand, she hailed a taxi and climbed into its warmth without apology. It was just too damn cold to walk to work.

"Where to?" The cab driver checked his mirrors before pulling out into the busy Pensacola Beach traffic.

"Fisher's Bookstore on Warrington."

"That building is still there? I heard they'd demolished it awhile back."

"I bought it. It's being renovated now and will be as good as new in no time."

Cathe had moved to Pensacola Beach, Florida from St. Augustine shortly after Craig's death. With nothing left for her back home, she'd decided to finish school and obtain her law degree somewhere that didn't remind her so much of what she'd lost. Besides, she'd spent several summers in Pensacola growing up and had always loved the place.

After retiring from family law where she'd been an attorney since graduating from college, she'd decided to purchase the old bookstore and restore it back to its original state.

"That's great. My wife has been buying books from there since she was a teenager," the cabbie remarked, weaving in and out of traffic.

Cathe smiled at his reflection in the rearview mirror. "Books are magical. They provide an escape from a world full of sorrow and pain."

The driver laughed. "Sounds like you love to read."

"More than anything."

Fisher's Bookstore came into view a moment later. Cathe paid the driver and climbed out into the blistering cold with keys in hand. She shivered and let herself inside, turning the Open sign on before making a beeline toward the old thermostat on the far wall.

It would take at least half an hour for the temperature in the room to raise enough to warm the place and another half an hour for her body to thaw.

The bell over the door chimed, letting her know she had an early customer. "I'll be right there!" she called, switching on the lights to the back of the store.

"Take your time. I'm just looking."

Making her way back to the front, Cathe turned the small key on the register until it clicked, unzipped the blue bag she'd removed from her purse, and took out an assortment of bills to fill the cash drawer.

She glanced up, acknowledging the woman perusing the romance aisle. "Good morning. Let me know if I can help you with anything."

"Thank you. Do you have any historical romance?"

"I sure do." Cathe meandered over and pointed out the meager selection. "Someone traded in a box of romance books yesterday, if you'd like to look through them."

"That's okay." The woman took down a book and flipped it over to read the back. "I'll take this one."

After paying for her purchase with a promise to return soon, the lady left.

Cathe picked up the box of books she'd gotten the day before and set it on the counter to price them before putting them on display.

What is it about romance novels that women find so appealing? She plucked one from the box, grinning at the gorgeous guy on the cover. *That would explain it.*

The day went by in a flurry of people looking for their next literary fix. Cathe could sympathize. She'd been addicted to reading since childhood, and it had stuck with her throughout her adult life as well. She read everything from memoirs to paranormal and everything in between.

Thunder rolled in the distance followed by a web of flashes streaking across the sky, signaling the impending arrival of the weather channel's predicted storm.

Cathe decided to close up early, hoping to make it out of the store and arrive home ahead of the rain.

The chime sounded on the door just as she made it to the thermostat on the back wall. "One second!" she yelled out, hoping to be heard over the thundering outside.

She switched off the heat and hurried back to the front. An elderly lady stood at the counter wearing a long wool coat that had seen better days, a tattered knitted hat, and a pair of thick glasses with lenses so dingy Cathe wondered how she could see out of them. Her shoes were well worn, and a piece of duct tape hung from the side of one.

Cathe's heart went out to her. "Sorry about that. May I help you?"

"Just returning a book," she rasped, keeping her head down.

Cathe cleared her throat. "The library is two blocks over, ma'am. This is Fisher's Bookstore."

The ancient old woman glanced toward the door. "I'll never make it there ahead of the rain. You'll see that it gets back to the library?"

Cathe peered down at the book and ran her fingers over the lettering on the light brown cover. A raised snake symbol rested just below the title, giving it an ominous appearance. *"Turn the Page,"* she read aloud. "How clever."

She carefully opened it to the first page and pulled out an old, faded library card. There were at least two dozen names written there, each one crossed through with ink. She glanced at the last name and the date listed next to it.

"Oh, wow, ma'am? Maybe you should just return it when you can. It was due back twenty-seven years ago."

When no answer came, Cathe looked up in time to see the woman exiting the store. "Wait!" she called, rushing around the counter and out the front door only to find the sidewalk empty. The tiny old lady had disappeared.

Cathe clutched the book to her chest and carried it back inside, carefully depositing it into her purse before shutting down the register. She grabbed her keys and switched off the lights on her way out. It would be dark soon, and with it another temperature drop. She made a mental note to return the book to the library on her way to work in the morning.

Catching another cab, she rode home in silence, staring out the window at the gathering clouds. How ironic that it would storm on the day of Craig's death, exactly as it had all those years ago. She hugged her purse to her chest...the heavy feel of the book inside felt oddly comforting.

A sprinkling of rain had begun to fall as Cathe arrived home. She quickly paid the driver before jumping from the cab and sprinting to her door. A cup of hot tea and a nice long bubble bath were just the things she needed.

* * * *

Cathe stepped from the tub and briskly dried off. She grabbed her favorite robe, wrapped herself in its fluffy softness, and trailed off to her bedroom to fall across her bed. The electric blanket she'd turned on before her bath assured her of its warmth.

The phone rang, but she ignored it, pulling the old book free of her purse and crawling under the covers to scope it out. It was probably her older sister calling to check on her anyway.

As far as families went, Cathe had a good one, and on any other day, she would have answered the call. Not today. Her emotions were riding too close to the surface, and the last thing she wanted to hear was, *Happy birthday.*

She took a deep breath and fought back the tears, well aware she should have stayed in therapy as recommended. Normal people moved on with their lives after the death of a loved one, but not Cathe. She grieved still, almost thirty years later.

Perhaps it was her fault for not letting go as she knew she should, and yet something deep inside refused to do that very thing. Her relationships had always suffered. It was like she couldn't give what was needed, always holding back a part of herself, the part where pain was created and born…her heart.

Thoughts of settling down and having children had been taken from her years ago, along with any notion of a happily ever after. No one could replace Craig, and no other child could ever take the place of the one she'd lost.

It wasn't that there weren't plenty of wonderful men in the world, Cathe thought with a sigh. They just didn't deserve to be saddled with someone that couldn't give them children or any kind of happiness.

Can't have it all. She glanced around her room, admiring the antiques and expensive furniture. She'd worked hard for everything she had and obviously didn't need a man to take care of things for her. No, she'd done just fine on her own…hadn't she?

Cathe shook off her thoughts and opened the book, skimming over the acknowledgements and publishing information to the first chapter. She was determined to lose herself in someone else's story for the night, no matter how briefly.

Two hours and many eye-watering moments later, Cathe found herself lost in the tale of the legendary, Lord Bryne Adair, the Earl of Hallensberg.

Originally from Westminster, London, Lord Adair had recently married Maria Alontra Charlotte of Mecklenburg-Strelitz's lady-in-waiting. Maria died of diphtheria shortly after giving birth to Adair's first-born son, and the child had passed not long after his mother.

Adair had been ordered by George William Frederick, King of England, to surrender his lands in exchange for a sizable castle in St. Augustine, Florida for the questioning of his allegiance.

When Adair refused, he'd been put on a ship with his belongings, and his castle had been burned to the ground.

Sources later revealed that Bryne Adair was thought to be the King's illegitimate brother, but the accusations couldn't be proven and the only evidence in existence was assumed to have been destroyed along with Adair's family home.

Bryne's father, the Marquess of Hallensberg, had taken his own life not long after Bryne's deportation to the Americas, leaving his title and legacy of shame to his only son.

Cathe yawned while blinking to keep her eyes open. She wondered how much of what she'd read so far was fact or fiction. The thought of losing a family home that had been passed down through generations on some bogus allegiance charge astounded her, but the loss of his wife and child was felt to her soul.

Her heart fluttered with the very description of the man as she continued to read. Why hadn't some other available female swooped in and claimed him after his wife's death? She wondered, shifting restlessly on the bed.

There had to be more to the story, she concluded, turning the page...

Chapter Two

Cathe jerked awake as the crack of lightning exploded somewhere nearby. She peered into the darkness, shivering against the cold. *The power must be out.*

Climbing from the bed, she glided her feet around in a circle in search of her slippers, only to come up empty. She'd obviously left them in the bathroom.

While holding both hands out in front of her, she inched across the room toward her dresser, hoping to find the candles she'd always kept in the top right-hand drawer.

"Shit," she cried, hopping around on one foot after slamming her toe into an immovable object. There shouldn't be anything in the middle of her floor.

More lightening struck, temporarily illuminating the room. Cathe froze. Her heart began to pound, and an overwhelming feeling of confusion paralyzed her brain. She wasn't in her bedroom or anyone else's that she recognized, and the woman staring back at her from an antique mirror…was far too young to be her.

She lifted trembling hands to her face, tracing her fingers over soft, smooth skin. How had she erased twenty years from her life in one night?

Panic took hold, making it hard to breathe. Her hands continued to shake as she wandered aimlessly toward a giant door she'd caught a glimpse of during the brief lightning strike.

She must be dreaming, she decided, feeling her way along a rough wall. That was it. She'd fallen asleep while reading the book the old woman had left in the store and was now in the throes of strange dream where she'd traveled back to her youth.

"Move, and I'll gut you like a pig," a man's voice growled in her ear. Something sharp pressed against her throat, and she bit back a scream.

This sure doesn't feel like any dream I've ever experienced. "Please don't hurt me. I'm lost, I swear. I have no idea how I came to be here, and if you will point me in the right direction, I will be out of your way this instant."

"What gibberish do you speak?" He pressed the sharp object more firmly against her skin.

"Gibberish?" She couldn't place his accent. It was prominently English with an American undertone, if that made sense, which it didn't. Maybe she imagined gibberish as well as spoke it.

"Move." He gave her a shove, pushing her forward, never easing up with his sharp weapon.

"I...I can't see. Look, there's been a huge mistake. I don't understand how I got here. Please, if you can just call me a cab, I'll be out of your hair and we can forget this ever happened."

The pressure suddenly disappeared from her throat, and she nearly dropped to her knees in relief.

"What is a cab?"

Cathe blinked. "Seriously?" When he didn't answer, she continued. "You know...a taxi. The yellow car that transfers people from one place to another."

"What manner of speech is this? I do not know what taxi you speak of."

What manner of speech? "It doesn't matter. I can get a ride home if you'd be so kind as to show me to the door."

A light from an oil lamp suddenly flickered and came to life, illuminating the room in a warm glow. Cathe turned to face the man whose bed she'd awoken in, and her breath caught.

His dark hair hung in waves, resting on the biggest pair of shoulders she'd ever seen. Full, sexy lips were twisted into a frown that didn't deter from their sexiness in the least. But it was his gunmetal-gray eyes that held her attention the most.

Too bad he happened to be the world's biggest asshole. "Where am I?"

"In my home," he growled, his beautiful eyes narrowed in suspicion.

"I'm not dreaming?" She glanced down at her smooth, young hands. This couldn't be happening to her, but it was. The evidence of it stared back at her in shocking affirmation.

"How did you get into my home?"

"I don't know how I got here or even who you are, for that matter."

"I am Lord Bryne Adair."

Cathe's heart stuttered. "Did...did you say Lord Bryne Adair?" She had to be dreaming or at the very least the star of someone's joke.

"Who sent you?" He leaned in close, and his sweet, warm breath fanned across her face.

"Please, listen." She gripped the lapels of her robe and pulled them together, effectively covering the upper swell of her breasts. "I fell asleep in my bed while reading this book about you. I don't know how I came to be here. You have to believe me."

"Trickery," he growled, gripping her arm. "I will deal with you in the morning. Now, walk."

"Where are we going?" His clean, fresh scent suddenly surrounded her, engulfing her in its unique essence. He smelled incredible.

"Tonight, you sleep with Ansel."

"What's an Ansel?" When he didn't answer, she tried again. "I don't want to sleep with Ansel. Please, there's been a mistake."

They entered a large hall made of stone with sconces attached holding small oil lamps that burned every fifteen feet along the wall.

"Is this some kind of a joke? Because if it is, it's not funny," Cathe whispered, taking in everything with a quick glance.

"You will return to William in the morning with a message." He squeezed her arm for emphasis. "The next witch he thinks to send here will be sent back without a head."

"You're hurting me," she ground out between clenched teeth. "The only William I know is my ten-year-old nephew, and I'd rather pass on becoming acquainted with your Ansel, thank you very much." Anger was quickly replacing her fear.

He turned her around and crossed his arms over his massive chest. "Where is this book you speak of?"

"I was reading it in bed before I fell asleep."

He grabbed a lamp from a holder on the wall and moved back into the bedroom, stopping at the foot of the bed. "There is no book."

Cathe followed close behind. "That's because this isn't my bed. Look. I don't know how I came to be here or even what this place is. All I know is that an old lady dropped a book off this evening in my store. There was a coiled snake on the cover beneath a title that read *Turn the Page*. That book was a two hundred and fifty year old story, and it was about you. You have to believe me."

He leaned down until their noses nearly touched. "Lies." Gripping her arm once more, he propelled her forward.

"Wait!" she cried, digging her heels in. "Just hear me out. My name is Catherine Grier, and I live at 2201 Santa Rosa Street in Pensacola Beach, Florida. I own Fisher's Book Store and my telephone number is 850-555-3003. Call the cops; they can verify who I am."

"I know not what a cop is or these numbers you refer to."

I'm in the Twilight Zone.

"I don't know what is going on, okay? I only know that I went to bed last night in the twenty-first century, reading that book, and I awoke to this." She threw her arms out in a wide arc. "I'm freaking out as much as you are."

He led her back to the hall and gave her a little shove. "Walk."

Cathe wondered if maybe she'd died in her sleep and this was purgatory. "Am I dead?"

"Not yet, but that could change depending on Ansel's mood."

"Listen. You don't want to do this Ansel thing. If you will show me to the door, I'll find my own way home."

He didn't answer, just continued to shove her forward.

They reached a flight of precarious-looking concrete stairs with no handrails, and the drop off the side had to be at least twenty feet in height.

Petrified, Cathe froze. She'd always been afraid of heights. "I can't."

He spun her around, bent, and threw her over his shoulder.

The wind rushed out of her on impact as his shoulder slammed into her abdomen. "Put me down," she gasped, squeezing her eyes shut in an attempt to block out the visual of the floor below.

He disregarded her plea and practically jogged down the incredibly steep steps.

"I'm going to be sick," she moaned, gripping his shirt for support.

The sting of his palm against her rear jerked her out of her nauseous state. "That hurt!" she yelled, slamming her fists against his back.

"Keep your mouth shut and do not think to be sick or perhaps I'll change my mind and keep you in my bed for a time before giving you to Ansel." He gently squeezed her ass for emphasis.

Cathe stilled. The feel of his warm palm caressing her bottom felt better than it should have, and it thoroughly pissed her off. "Take your hands off me this instant, you Neanderthal. And you can go on knowing that I will be pressing charges."

The deep rumble of his laughter further enraged her, but she kept it to herself. There would be plenty of time later to watch him suffer behind bars.

They arrived at the bottom of the stairs, and he set her on her feet. "In there." He pointed to a half-open door with a fireplace burning in the back.

"Please listen to—"

"Go!" he roared, cutting her off.

Cathe ran into the room without a backward glance, jumping at the sound of the door slamming behind her. She spun around and reached for the doorknob, only to find a strange contraption resembling a brass spoon resting above a skeleton keyhole.

She drew back her fist, preparing to pound the walls down if necessary. Hopefully she could make enough noise to draw someone's attention. Someone other than asshole Adair, that was.

"I wouldn't do that if I was you." A nasally voice drifted from somewhere nearby. "The master don't like that sorta thing."

Cathe sucked in a breath and spun to scan the room. "Who's there?"

A tall, lanky man came limping from the shadows, holding a candle in one hand and a rope in the other. "Get away from the door."

Nausea rolled once again as she caught a whiff of his stench. The guy obviously didn't believe in bathing. "If it's money that you want, I have plenty of it. I just need to run to my house and get my purse. I can write you a check or—"

"Shut up," he snarled, moving closer, setting the candle on a lopsided table.

"Please. You have to help me. I'm not supposed to be here. There's been some kind of a mistake. I—"

He gripped the back of her head with one hand and covered her mouth with the other. The rope he held dug into her scalp while his putrid scent invaded her senses, triggering her gag reflex.

Her sudden bout of dry heaves forced him to take a step back. "What's wrong with ya, woman?"

She couldn't answer as another heave caused her eyes to water and her mouth to tighten with the effort of holding onto her earlier dinner. She shook her head instead.

He grabbed a wooden chair from nearby and forced her to sit as he jerked her wrists behind her back and bound them with the rope he held in his hands. "What he send ya down here for? Catch ya stealin or somethin?"

"He's crazy. I didn't do anything wrong, but he wouldn't listen."

"Well, I ain't listenin' either. So shut your trap before I shut if for ya."

"Please untie my hands. I have no weapons on me." She pulled at the restraints, but there was no give to the ropes. "Why are you doing this to me?"

The man known as Ansel left the room for a few minutes. She could hear voices outside the door and recognized the deep timbre of Bryne Adair's.

Ansel returned carrying a dirty strip of cloth, and Cathe's nerves ran up her stomach straight into her head. "What is that for? Surely you're not going to—"

A scream trapped in her throat as the nasty material was suddenly stuffed into her mouth, cutting off her words. The unwelcome gag reflex abruptly appeared once more.

The tall, lanky guy stepped around the chair, stopping in front of her. "It don't matter much to me who ya are. It only matters who the master thinks ya are."

Cathe pleaded with him through her eyes, the only weapon she had left since he'd restrained her arms and gagged her. She might as well be pleading with a stump for all it got her. If she truly was in a bad dream, she'd give anything to wake up right now.

Chapter Three

Bryne Adair threw open the shutters and stared out his bedroom window at the inky sky beyond. Images of his intruder plagued his mind, making sleep unobtainable. She'd said her name was Catherine Grier from Pensacola.

What was a young, blonde female doing in a place occupied mostly by Spanish and Indians?

She didn't strike him as a courtesan or even a common street girl, and though her hair hung loose around her shoulders and boasted different shades of the same color, it looked right on her.

He did like that she didn't make her face up with kohl and powders as most of the women of the ton did. Of course they weren't in England, and judging by her strange talk, she wasn't from there either.

Witch. That had to be it. The king had sent a witch to seduce him in hopes of obtaining his hidden documents—the evidence of his birth thought to have been destroyed along with his castle back in England.

Bryne ran a hand through his hair as he stripped out of his clothes and climbed into his oversized bed. He'd have plenty of time on the morrow to get the answers he sought after a good night's rest.

He was tired, tired of fighting and tired of politics, but most of all tired of not taking what was his. His thoughts drifted to his sister back in Westminster; if not for the threats against her life and the lives of her children, he would have stayed and risked being burned along with his castle.

* * * *

Cathe realized the moment that Ansel returned. His smell preceded him into the room, demanding her notice whether she lifted her head or not.

She bit the inside of her cheek to keep from crying out as he wrapped a hand in her hair, yanked her head up, and pulled the nasty cloth loose from her mouth.

"Who sent you?" His breath settled over her like a rotted corpse, suffocating her.

"No one sent me. I told you already. I woke up here," she reiterated, jerking her face to the side.

"I heard ya the first time, but I ain't buyin' it."

"Please. I'm telling you the truth." Cathe noticed his clothes. The shirt he wore was open at the collar with ruffles running the length of the front. Though dingy, it had obviously been white at some point and was now in desperate need of some bleach. His pants were too short, and he wore no socks with his shoes.

He released her bound hands. "I'll get the truth from ya one way or another."

"What are you going to do?" Anxiety tightened her gut once more.

"Get up," he demanded, yanking her arms at an awkward angle.

Cathe gritted her teeth. "You don't have to manhandle me. I can stand on my own."

"Get goin' then." He shoved her through the open door to the left of a massive dining room with an oversized table situated near an enormous fireplace.

Dark-colored drapes hung from long, narrow windows, and beautiful rugs were resting haphazardly around the floor.

"What is this place?"

"Shut your mouth and keep movin'."

They came to a pair of giant wooden doors with golden handles and a sliding bar for a locking mechanism. Cathe barely had time to take in their antique beauty before the doors were thrown open and she was pushed outside into the chilly winter wind.

The sight that greeted her as she stumbled down the concrete steps stole her breath. She was standing in a courtyard surrounded by a huge wall with cannons embedded in the sides at least every thirty feet.

"What in the world…?" The building was square in shape with stairs that ran along the inside, leading up to a ledge that bordered a massive wall. It had to be the most intimidating structure she'd ever seen. "It's a castle," she breathed in awe.

"Course it's a castle. What else would it be? Master thinks you're a witch. What ya got to say for yourself?"

A nervous giggle bubbled up. "A witch? Your master? What century do you think this is?" she asked with a sarcastic tone. "Look. My name is Catherine Grier, I live in Pensacola Beach, and I was born in Arlington, Texas. Do an online search and see for yourself. I'm no witch. "

Ansel spun her around, his facial features twisted into a frown. "I never heard of Arlington, Texas, ya batshit-crazy witch." He pointed to a pillory erected at the other end of the courtyard. "That's where you'll be stayin' for the rest of the day. Or 'til ya can admit the truth."

Cathe braced to run, but he grabbed hold of her arm and twisted it behind her back. "Ain't gonna happen, witch lady." He propelled her forward, stopping in front of the medieval-looking contraption. "Now step up."

"I can't be locked in that thing," Cathe pleaded. "You don't understand. I'm extremely claustrophobic. I'll die if you put me in there."

"Jump up there," he barked, twisting her arm to the point where she thought surely it would break.

She stumbled onto the platform, scanning the grounds for anyone who might help her. "Please."

He ignored her plea, forcing her head and wrists into the pillory and snapping it closed. The loud click that followed cemented her fate.

"Help!"

"Yell all ya want. Ain't nobody gonna help ya." He strolled back toward the castle doors, disappearing from her sight before she could process what had just happened.

* * * *

Cathe couldn't feel her feet. Panic had long since disappeared and in its place settled acceptance. She was going to die out here in the middle of a courtyard, in a strange place without her underwear.

It had been a long-standing joke growing up to always wear underwear in case you were in an accident, yet here she was bent in half, freezing to death in full-on commando.

Her legs gave out, and she momentarily sagged, sending shooting pain through her arms and neck before locking her knees once more. That was the intended torture of the device, she assumed. It involved physical as well as mental anguish.

She turned her head and studied her right hand once again. The youthful appearance of her skin astounded her. How was it possible? Had the book she'd fallen asleep reading the night before been cursed? She didn't believe in curses or magic…so how had she come to be here?

Footsteps sounded nearby, and Cathe strained to see around the sharp angles of wood on her torture device. "Hello?" When no answer came, she tried again. "Can you hear me? Please. I just want to ask you a question."

"You're that witch. I ain't supposed to talk to ya." A woman stepped into Cathe's line of vision, wearing a black and white dress that flowed to her ankles and an apron tied around her waist. Her blonde hair was tucked up under a frilly white cap that had seen better days.

"I'm not a witch. I'm just lost," Cathe muttered, thinking that the woman would be pretty after a pair of tweezers, a brush, and a good scrubbing.

"That ain't what Ansel says. He says you're soft in the head and don't know what century it is."

With an inward sigh, Cathe pasted on a smile. "Okay, then why don't you tell me what year we are in?"

The woman's head tilted to the side, and she stared back at Cathe as if she truly were addled. "This is the month of February, 1767."

Cathe's heart stuttered and her vision faded. The ground tilted momentarily before righting itself. "Did you say 1767?"

The woman nodded. "Seems to me that you're insane. They should've put ya down instead of displayin' ya out here for all to see. Inhumane, if ya ask me." She meandered off before Cathe could question her further.

It's 1767? So it's true. I fell asleep reading that book and awoke in a different time. But how is that possible?

If she'd have been told that time travel was possible and someday she would be a victim of it, she would have thought that person crazy. Hell, she doubted her own sanity at this point. But here she was in the center of a courtyard locked in a pillory in the eighteenth century, freezing her ass off.

Her teeth continued to chatter and not just from the cold. Something inside that book held the power to send her back in time nearly two hundred and fifty years, and if she didn't find it soon, she had a feeling she'd be stuck here...if she didn't die first.

* * * *

Bryne Adair wandered nude over to the window just after daybreak when the fog rolling in from the Matanzas Bay was at its thickest. He watched as the mist drifted by, reflecting off the glow of a distant lighthouse.

St. Augustine wasn't his home, but he'd grown fond of the place with its warm summer winds and tolerable winters.

He stared out over the water, admiring its beauty and serenity before settling his gaze on the sexy blonde witch restrained in his courtyard. His cock hardened with the memory of her scent...his hand on her ass.

With a growl, he marched back toward his bed and pulled the thick golden cord hanging from the ceiling to signal a servant.

Betty rushed in almost immediately, tucking a stray blonde curl back into place and pinching her cheeks. Her hair color wasn't as bright as the witch's, he noticed.

"What can I do for ya, Master," she purred, sashaying across the room with her feet bare and her bosom spilling out over the top of her nightgown. Her eyes lit up with desire as she took in his naked form.

Bryne scarcely noticed, his thoughts too wrapped up in the deceptive female freezing to death in his courtyard.

"Have my bath drawn," he ordered, turning to stare out the window once more.

The maid sidled up behind him. "Want some company, Master?"

"No, thank you," he muttered dismissively, never taking his gaze from his prisoner. "Have Miss Grier brought to my room also."

"Miss Grier?" the maid questioned, backing up a step.

"Yes. She's locked in the pillory. Bring her to me."

"But—"

"Now, Betty."

She ran from the room without another word, and for that, Bryne was grateful. Out of all the servants he employed, she was the most talkative one.

Bernie and Walt came in a few minutes later, followed by a couple of teenage boys carrying pails of hot water, which they promptly poured into the tub.

Bryne thanked them and clapped Bernie on the shoulder. "Congratulations on the baby boy."

"Oh, thank ya, Master. His name is Wiley," Bernie proudly announced with his chest puffed out more than usual.

"Wiley. That's a good name," Bryne praised, stepping back as more servants entered with pails of hot water.

"It's my wife's dead father's name, Sire."

"Well, it's a good name, Bernie." Bryne waved his hand at the rest of the servants. "That will be all. I'll ring if I need any further assistance."

"Yes, my Lord," the men chorused as they filed out one by one.

Chapter Four

Footsteps echoed off the surrounding walls, making it difficult for Cathe to gauge which direction they came from.

She shifted her gaze toward the main door of the castle and noticed a blonde woman dressed in a flimsy nightgown. Her shoes were laced up to the ankles, and she seemed to be wearing some kind of hose. Her hair was hidden under a pink cloth cap, and the tops of her breasts threatened to bounce free with every step she took.

The look on her face reeked of anger, and the closer she got the more it seemed directed at Cathe.

"It's your lucky day," the woman sneered, stopping next to Cathe with a set of skeleton keys.

Releasing the lock, the stranger lifted the heavy wood, freeing Cathe's hands and neck. "Come with me." The blonde turned to go without waiting to see if her prisoner would follow.

Cathe stumbled forward before falling to her hands and knees. Pebbles and dirt dug into her skin, wrenching a cry from her.

"Get up." The woman gripped Cathe by the hair and yanked, forcing her to her feet.

It took everything Cathe had to keep from crying out in pain, but she'd be damned if she would give the bitch the pleasure of hearing it.

"Mornin', Betty!" a man leading a horse toward a stable yelled out.

"How ya doin', Walt?" Betty responded with a wink.

The guy muttered something that Cathe couldn't understand before disappearing inside the stables.

"Go on," Betty demanded, shouldering Cathe up the steps and inside the castle doors. "Up the stairs."

Cathe's stomach tightened in dread. She was once again going to have to brave those steep, horrifying stairs.

The climb to the top took forever in Cathe's mind with Betty following closely on her heels. She kept expecting the strangely dressed woman to push her off the higher up they went. Not that she would feel it, she silently acknowledged. She'd probably lost her feet to frostbite.

The two of them finally emerged onto the top landing and entered the same hallway that Cathe had been in the night before. *Maybe Mr.*

Adair has come to his senses and decided to let me go.

Betty knocked on his bedroom door before throwing it open. "In there." She elbowed Cathe in the back, forcing her over the threshold.

The sight that greeted Cathe as she stumbled into his room shocked her speechless. If she were a cartoon character, she'd be manually rolling her tongue up off the floor for the next ten minutes.

"Thank you, Betty. That'll be all for now," Bryne ordered, his gaze zeroing in on Cathe.

"My Lord," Betty bit out before turning on her heel and pulling the door shut behind her as she left.

"Take off the robe." His deep voice penetrated Cathe's shocked brain, but did nothing to steer her eyes in a different direction.

Cathe stared, her gaze glued to him in stunned disbelief and more than a little curiosity. A dark dusting of hair spread across his overly wide chest and ran down his washboard abs to settle above the most impressive cock she'd ever seen.

The sheer length of it alone was astounding, but it was the width that intimidated her.

"You— You're not wearing clothes," she stuttered before clearing her throat to try again. "Why are you naked?"

His answering grin was more daunting than his nudity. "I was about to take a bath." He tilted his head toward the tub. "Join me."

Cathe's face grew hot with embarrassment. "I'd rather not."

He took a step toward her. "It wasn't a request."

"I realize that you were born in barbaric times and are used to getting what you want, but I'm not one of your servants, and I'm certainly not bathing with you."

He raised an eyebrow while continuing toward her. "Barbaric times?"

She forced her gaze upward to no avail; his imposing cock was still within her view. "Could you cover yourself, please?"

Taking her by the wrist, he gently pulled her forward until her body bumped into his. "Either you remove the robe, or I'll remove it for you. Do not think to fight me on this and don't bother to scream as there is no one to help you, witch."

Cathe's chest hurt, whether from chills or fear she wasn't sure. "You're going to rape me?"

A muscle ticked along his jaw. "I do not force women against their will."

"It's against my will to get in that tub with you."

He leaned down until their noses touched. "I vow before the day's end, you will beg me to take you."

"Then you're in for a rude awakening. I have never, nor will I ever beg a man for anything."

He slowly ran his tongue along his lower lip. "You will beg," he rumbled, staring at her mouth. "All night."

Cathe couldn't move. His gunmetal-gray eyes hypnotized her, holding her in a spell she couldn't seem to break.

"Get in the bath before the water grows cold." He pulled her sash free and opened her robe.

"Don't." She grabbed for the lapels, but he was faster, yanking the robe down her arms and off before she could finish her sentence.

Covering her breasts with her arms, Cathe quickly stepped over the side of the tub and sank down into the warm water. Her shivering stopped almost instantly. "How dare you."

"Slide forward," he demanded, entering behind her. He sat, pulling her back against his front. "Now relax against me and use my body heat to remove your chill."

"If you're trying to demean me in some way, you've made your point," she bit out between clenched teeth.

He picked up a bottle of shampoo that smelled of strawberries sitting next to the tub. "Dunk."

"What?"

"Wet your hair."

"I can wash my—"

Her mouth filled with water as he gripped her shoulders, forcing her head under. She came up sputtering. "Your butt water got in my mouth."

Booming laughter startled her, and she stared straight ahead, afraid to move. It sounded rusty as if laughing was something he rarely did.

He finally calmed. "Butt water. I like the way you think."

Cathe sat completely still while he poured some of the strawberry liquid onto his palm and began massaging it into her scalp. "You wear your hair as a courtesan and yet you do not act as one."

"A courtesan? You mean a whore?" She couldn't believe she was sitting naked in a tub with an equally naked man that she didn't know, having a conversation about prostitutes.

"Tell me how you came to be here, Catherine Grier. Speak the truth, and I will consider sparing your life."

The truth. Yeah, like he's going to accept the truth. "You wouldn't believe me if I told you."

"Try me."

Here goes nothing. "Okay. My name really is Catherine Grier. My friends call me Cathe." She paused.

"Go on."

"I'm not a witch, nor do I know exactly how I ended up here."

"I too am puzzled as to how you managed to infiltrate my home."

"Not here as in your castle. I meant here in your century."

The hands massaging her head subsided. "You say that you are not a witch, and yet you claim to be from another time. How are the two different?"

How indeed? Cathe couldn't think past the feeling of his hands in her hair and his stomach touching her back.

Her insides grew weak with the feel of his erection pressing against her ass. Words seemed to escape her.

pg. 43

He tilted his hips slightly and brought his lips close to her ear. "You like that, little witch?"

She could only moan as he slid his hands down her neck, over her shoulders, under her arms and around to her breasts to gently squeeze, softly pinching her nipples between his fingers. "I want to bury myself inside you so deep you won't know where you end and I begin."

"Adair..."

He ignored her. "I want you wrapped around me as I fuck your sweet heat until you're begging me to let you come."

His palms coasted down her stomach, and Cathe held her breath in anticipation of having him touch her where she ached the most.

"My Lord?" a voice called from outside the bedroom door.

Cathe stiffened in mortification. What the hell was wrong with her? She'd almost caved and had sex with Bryne Adair in a giant tub sitting in the center of his bedroom, in a castle...in the eighteenth century, no less.

A low growl came from her bath companion. "What is it, Bennie?"

The door opened, and a short, skinny man with salt-and-pepper hair stepped into the room.

Cathe sank as far down into the water as she could get.

"Sorry to bother, my Lord, but you have a visitor," Bennie announced, keeping his eyes downcast.

Bryne wrapped his arms around her, keeping her hidden from view. "Who is it?"

"A messenger of the king, my Lord."

"See to it that he is made comfortable, Bennie. I will be right down."

"Very good, Sire." With a quick bow, the servant ducked out the door, pulling it shut behind him.

"I will have clothes brought to you shortly. Stay in my room and wait for my return. I am not finished with you, temptress."

Stepping from the tub, he grabbed a towel lying on the foot of his bed, and Cathe got a glimpse of his well-defined ass before.

She quickly rinsed her hair and picked up the soap sitting next to the tub to finish her bath. "How long will you be gone?"

"Not long. I'll return as soon as I can. We have much to discuss." He strayed over to the dresser in a pair of tight pants that laced up in the front. Muscles bunched and moved across his shoulders, and Cathe found herself hypnotized by the water droplets trickling down his back. "I need to go home."

He was suddenly in her face with her chin in his hand. "A guard will be positioned in the hall with orders to secure you in the pillory once more if you think to leave. Do I make myself clear?"

"Perfectly," she ground out, staring at him with as much contempt as she could feign.

"That's better." He leaned in and kissed her before she could stop him, straightened, and dragged on a shirt.

Cathe was seething with anger by the time he stepped into his boots. How dare he touch her against her will?

It wasn't completely against her will, she admitted to herself. What had taken place in the bathtub had been consensual, and damn her for wanting it again.

She stood and scanned the room for a towel the second he disappeared into the hallway, but found only the one he'd recently used lying beside the tub. Snatching it up, she brought it to her nose.

His scent was an aphrodisiac to her starved senses. It had been years since she'd had sex and never with someone that smelled as good as him. Or was as well endowed for that matter, she thought with a blush.

The door abruptly opened, and Betty stormed inside carrying a bundle of clothes in her arms, leaving Cathe to throw the towel around her body and promptly step from the tub. "Have you ever heard of knocking?"

An agitated- looking Betty thrust the clothes at her. "The master sent me up here with these. If ya ask me, he should have borrowed some of Walt's boy's clothes for ya. Ya ain't nothin' but bones and titties as far as I can tell."

"No one asked you, Betsy," Cathe shot back, silently fuming.

"It's Betty," she retorted with her hands on her hips.

"Betsy, Betty. Whatever. And if you ask *me, you* could stand a good bathing." Cathe gripped the maid's shoulders and shoved her over the rim of the tub without thinking.

Betty came up spitting and sputtering, a horrified look on her face. Her bottom lip began to tremble and tears sprang to her eyes.

Cathe instantly regretted her outburst. "I'm so sorry, Betty. Here, let me help you." She extended her hand toward the trembling maid.

"Leave me be."

"Please?" Cathe knelt next to the tub, keeping her palm outstretched. "I don't know what came over me."

The maid stared back at her in suspicion.

pg. 47

"No tricks, I swear."

Betty tentatively slid her palm against Cathe's before wrapping her fingers around her wrist...and giving it a yank. Cathe wound up face-planting into the giant tub alongside the disgruntled maid.

She sat up with a gasp and pushed her wet hair back from her eyes. "Betsy!"

"It's Betty," she snapped, splashing more water into Cathe's face.

Too shocked to speak, Cathe stared back at her in stunned disbelief until the humor of the situation finally sank in. An unexpected giggle burst free and then another.

Betty soon joined in, and the room was instantly filled with side-splitting laughter.

Cathe laughed until her ribs hurt, until tears of mirth dripped from the corners of her eyes. There, amidst a tub full of used bath water, in a castle from the eighteenth century...an oddly, unorthodox friendship was born.

Chapter Five

Lord Adair pinched the bridge of his nose and read the king's message once again. "The gall of that man," he growled, lifting his gaze and pinning the messenger with a stare usually reserved for his enemy.

"'Tis not his fault, my Lord," Walt intervened from behind Bryne's shoulder.

"I know where the fault lies." Adair shifted in his seat and jerked his chin toward the nervous messenger. "See that he has food and a place to bed for the night. And Walt?"

"Sire?"

"Have some food sent to my room for our guest also."

"You're going to feed the witch, Sire?"

Bryne ground his teeth in frustration. It wasn't in his nature to explain himself to the help or anyone else for that matter. "Aye. Her name is Miss Grier."

"Yes, my Lord. Will ya be planning on sendin' a reply to His Majesty?"

"Perhaps," Bryne responded, glancing at his quill. "It would seem the king has decided to visit our neighboring lands."

Walt's eyes grew huge. "Ya mean the king is here, Sire?"

Adair nodded. "It appears that he's called a meeting with Governor Grant, and my presence has been requested."

"But he's not to be trusted, my Lord."

Bryne was all too aware of the king's shortcomings. "That'll be all, Walt."

"Sire." The servant bowed and motioned for the messenger to follow him toward the castle doors.

Taking a deep breath, Bryne grabbed the quill and penned a response to the king.

Most High and Mighty Sovereign,

In obedience to Your Majesty's commands and with submission to superior judgment, I hereby confirm the attendance of myself along with my second-in-command at Fort Matanzas on the tenth day of February, 1767.

Your obedient servant,

Lord Bryne Adair III, Earl of Hallensberg.

Bryne folded the letter, heated the wax, and sealed it with his family crest. He would have it sent back to the king first thing in the morning.

Stretching his legs out in front of him, he leaned back in his chair and let his mind drift to the bath he'd taken with the witch.

His cock grew hard with the memory of her delicious scent, her skin against his, the feel of her hair in his hands. He wondered what she would taste like, if she would arch beneath him when he took her. And he would take her, he silently vowed, shifting in his seat. *Soon...*

"My Lord?" Walt's sudden reappearance brought Bryne out of his reverie.

Bryne quickly sat up and swung his legs under the table in an attempt to hide his erection. "What is it, Walt?"

"I took the food to your room just like ya told me to, but the woman ain't there."

"What?" Bryne growled, jumping to his feet. "Who let her out?"

"Weren't me, Sire," the servant called out to Adair's retreating back. But Bryne was no longer listening. His witch had somehow escaped from under his nose, and that bothered him more than he wanted to admit.

"Close the gate," Bryne barked over his shoulder. "No one leaves or enters the grounds without my knowledge. Understood? No one."

"Yes, Sire."

Bryne took the stairs two at a time to the top-floor landing. He burst through the door to his room only to find it empty. Puddles of water surrounded the tub as if there had been a struggle.

He picked up Cathe's robe lying in a heap at the foot of his bed and brought it to his nose.

Her delicious scent invaded his senses, bringing to life feelings he'd forgotten existed.

"Where is Betty, Walt?" he asked the servant now stumbling out of breath through the door.

"I ain't seen her since she brung the clothes up here for the witch, my Lord."

"Her name is Catherine Grier, and you will address her as Miss Grier."

"Yes, Sire."

"I want you to go over every nook and cranny of this castle until she is found. Check the servants' quarters also."

Walt bowed and scurried from the room without a backward glance.

Bryne wandered over to the window in a daze. What was it about the woman that toyed with his mind? He shouldn't care what happened to her or where she went, but he did.

A thought suddenly occurred to him, and he turned from the window in a rage. She'd vanished shortly after the arrival of the king's messenger. That was it, he seethed, gripping the handle of his sword. Catherine Grier, the beautiful witch of his dreams, worked for the king.

Was she sleeping with him, allowing him inside her creamy white body? Bryne shook off his thoughts before the fury now sneaking its way in suddenly consumed him and forced him to ride to General Grant's in search of the king's head.

Why did it enrage him so much to think of her with George? It wasn't as if Bryne had known her for any length of time or that she'd betrayed him in some way. She'd awoken in his bed only the night before with an insane tale of being from the future.

Bryne preferred her futuristic story over her being the king's paramour. Hell, he'd take her as a witch...anything but George's mistress.

He should be glad she was gone and not his problem any longer. At least she hadn't found what she'd been sent to retrieve. Or had she? he wondered, stalking over to his dresser and pulling it forward to step behind it.

Bryne slid his hand along the wall, feeling his way over the rocky surface until he found what he sought. There amid the layers of uneven stones lay a loose, flat rock. Applying gentle pressure, he tugged the rock free and retrieved the folded parchment tucked safely inside.

Relief was short-lived however with the realization that the witch would go back to the king empty-handed and more than likely lose her life.

After returning the document to its hidden home and replacing the stone, Bryne pushed the dresser back against the wall and ran from the room.

"Ansel!" he roared, descending the stairs and storming toward the castle doors.

The lanky, unwashed servant staggered into the great hall with huge eyes and his bushy white hair standing on end. "My Lord?"

"I need a dozen soldiers saddled and ready to go within half an hour."

"Yes, my Lord." The servant followed his master into the courtyard.

"Ansel?"

"Sire?"

"I'll be riding Reaper. See that he's set."

"Yes, my Lord."

Bryne glanced at the pillory where Cathe had been held in the freezing weather earlier that morning, and his stomach clenched. His head told him that she was a witch and needed to be destroyed, but his heart cried out against it. Perhaps she'd cast a spell on him, blinding him to her evil. He shook his head, questioning his sanity...or lack thereof.

"Haskell," Bryne called before rapping his knuckles on the man's door. "Virgil, open up."

"Is everything okay, my Lord?" Virgil Haskell pulled the door open and stepped back to allow Adair entrance.

"I need you to ride with me to Governor Grant's."

"Virgil's eyebrows shot up. "Of course, my Lord."

"Enough with the formalities... You're like a brother to me."

"As you are to me," Virgil concurred. "What's at the Governor's, and how many weapons do we need?"

Bryne took a deep breath and rubbed the back of his neck. How was he supposed to explain the witch to his second-in-command? "It's not *what's* at the Governors', Virgil; it's *who* is at the Governor's."

Another eyebrow lift from Virgil stretched Bryne's patience. "Ready yourself. I'll explain on the way."

* * * *

Cathe fought a yawn as she sat on the seawall and let her feet dangle above the water. She smiled at the minnows fighting over the bread crumbs that she and Betty had recently fed them. "This feels like home."

Betty's short, plump legs swung next to Cathe's. "Where is your home?"

"I live in Pensacola Beach now, but I'm originally from St. Augustine."

"Are ya really from the future?" The maid's eyes were comically huge.

Cathe simply nodded, turning her gaze to the sky. "And I need to return soon."

"How ya suppose to get back?"

How was she supposed to go home? "I wish I knew."

"Well, how'd ya come to be here?"

Cathe recited the day's events that led up to her arrival in Lord Asshole's bed. "And he won't listen to a thing I say. He thinks I'm a witch sent from the king to spy on him."

"Well, are ya?"

"Am I what?"

"A witch?"

A laugh bubbled up. "Only in the mornings before I have my coffee."

Betty stared at her for a long moment before chuckling also. "I get it." She continued to study Cathe's face until it was beginning to grow uncomfortable.

"What?" Cathe queried. "Do I have something in my teeth?"

"No, course not. I just didn't know wellborn ladies drank coffee, is all."

"Well born? Listen, Betty. I came from the twenty-first century, and in my time, we are all equal. There is no wellborn versus lowborn unless you're considered royalty, then you'd find yourself floating in Asshole's boat, thinking like Asshole, and looking like the Asshole."

Betty burst into a fit of giggles. "Does my Lord know ya call him Asshole?"

"I still have my head, don't I?"

"That ya do." Betty grinned. "For now anyway." She pushed to her feet and extended her hand. "We better get ya back before I get my head lopped off with yours."

Cathe accepted Betty's outstretched palm and stood. "Where can I get something to eat around here? My stomach feels like it's eating my backbone."

"I have some stew simmerin'. You're welcome to eat with me."

"Thank you, Betty. That sounds divine."

* * * *

"Why are we taking only a dozen men on this excursion? It could be a trap," Virgil pointed out on his way through the gate.

"If George wanted me dead, I most likely would be by now. I have something he wants, something of great value to him, and as long as it is in my possession, we are in no danger of the grave."

"He could have you arrested and tortured for said information, Sire. You're not immortal, you realize. As much as you seem to think you are."

"Easy, Haskell...I can still kick your ass without breaking a sweat."

Virgil glanced over at his friend and overlord. "You wish, old man. You forget I am far younger than you."

"By only a month or two," Bryne corrected. "Now close that hole beneath your nose and ride. We are wasting daylight."

Virgil Haskell was a giant of a man. He and Bryne had become friends in their youth and remained the closest of friends today. Haskell had saved Adair's ass on more than one occasion, and Bryne trusted him with his life.

They had barely made it a mile outside the gate when the sound of a horse whinnying could be heard coming from the trees. Bryne lifted his arm to halt his men. "Stay where you are," he ordered before turning to his second. "Virgil, come with me."

Bryne steered his horse to the water's edge, following the seawall to a clump of trees in the distance. Dismounting, he tethered his stallion to a low-lying limb and slowly crept toward a saddled mare that carried his brand.

"Looks like one of yours," Virgil whispered from close behind. Bryne wouldn't have heard the guy's approach if he hadn't been expecting it. For someone of his size, Virgil moved as quietly as the natives.

It was said a Mocama Indian could sneak up on a man standing in a bed of dried leaves. Bryne was inclined to believe it after watching Virgil in action.

Neither of them spoke as they crept silently through the trees, coming to a stop at the sound of feminine voices.

"Are ya gonna tell me if ya lay with my Lord or not?"

"Lay with him? You mean have sex with him?"

Adair recognized Catherine's voice immediately. He glanced at Virgil and put a finger to his lips, eager to hear the witch's response. He didn't have long to wait.

"You couldn't pay me enough money to lay with him."

"But why not? He's a comely one, and have ya seen the size of his rod?"

Bryne grinned at the maid's description of his manly parts.

"It didn't impress me in the least," Cathe shot back. "And I'd rather have sex with a man less endowed than a full-blown asshole."

A soft snicker behind him assured Adair that Virgil had heard the insult also. He threw a dirty look over his shoulder before storming from his hidden spot beneath the trees. "It's not enough to be merely an asshole, but I'm to be a full-blown one also."

Cathe took a step back, her eyes huge in her face. "Adair. I didn't hear you come up."

"So it would seem."

"We was just headin' back in, my Lord," Betty interjected. "The miss here is hungry."

"You may return home, Betty. Miss Grier will be riding in with me," Bryne stated, daring either of them to argue.

"Yes, my Lord." Betty shot Cathe an apologetic look before clambering off to find her horse.

Chapter Six

Cathe couldn't believe Lord Asshole had just dismissed her new friend as if she were nothing. The world sure had come a long way from the eighteenth century, she thought, staring into Adair's arrogant eyes. He would never survive in her time...not with his attitude. "Must you treat people as if they are beneath you?"

He tilted his head to the side as if confused by her question. "You refer to Betty? She is a servant."

His matter-of-fact tone further enraged Cathe. "Because you were born in caveman times and clearly don't know any better, I'm going to let that disgusting comment slide." She stepped around him and nearly walked into a tank of a man.

"You must be the witch." The tank smiled, showing off a dimple. "I am Virgil. It is a pleasure to meet you." He took hold of Cathe's hand and brought it to his lips, brushing a kiss across her knuckles.

Cathe easily returned his smile. He had a friendly face and warm demeanor. "Nice to meet you too, Virgil. I'm Catherine, but you can call me Cathe."

Bryne suddenly took her by the arm. "It is time to go."

"Come on, old man. I was only becoming acquainted with the lady. I will see that she gets home safely."

"She rides with me," Bryne growled, yanking her closer to his body.

Virgil held up both hands. "I surrender for now. Perhaps on the morrow we can—"

"Stand down, Haskell." The quiet finality of Adair's voice sent shivers down Cathe's back.

"As you wish, my Lord," Haskell responded with a wink. "I will see you at dinner."

Adair visibly relaxed. "Cathe and I will be dining alone this evening."

"Until next time then." Blowing a kiss in Cathe's direction, Virgil digressed back to the trees.

Cathe snatched her arm from Bryne's grip. "Let's get something straight, *my Lord*. You do not own me, and you most certainly cannot and will not dictate who I see or become friends with. Understood?"

He bent until his nose was an inch from hers. A move he seemed to do a lot. "If I find out that you have touched or been alone with Virgil Haskell or any other man for that matter,

I will spank your bottom until you cannot sit down and then permanently lock you in the tower. *Understood?*"

"I'd like to see you try," she shot back and stormed off in the direction Virgil had recently departed in.

Bryne caught up to her in three easy steps, bent, and locked his arm behind her thighs before throwing her over his shoulder once again.

"Put me down, damn it," she demanded through clenched teeth.

Easily mounting his horse, he slid into the saddle and tugged her down in front of him until she sat on his lap with her legs hanging off to one side.

She could smell his unique scent, and her stomach fluttered. She hated that he had that effect on her.

The heat from his body penetrated her clothes, stealing her very breath. Cathe wanted to bury her face in his neck and breathe him in, but she couldn't. She needed to remember that he was a barbaric asshole with barbaric tendencies. She inched as far away from him as the saddle would allow.

"Be still, damn it. You're killing me." He tightened his hold on her.

"You think this is comfortable for me? Your sword handle is digging into my thigh," she snapped, attempting to put some distance between them.

"That is not all you will feel digging into your thigh if you do not stop moving."

Cathe stilled, realizing the implication of his words. It wasn't that she didn't find him attractive; on the contrary, the man reeked of sexy. No, she was more worried about losing her heart to him and then leaving him behind when she returned home.

He shifted in the saddle, and Cathe glanced down between their bodies at the thick outline of his erection. A soft gasp escaped her.

"Damn you, witch," he growled, wrapping a hand in her hair and pulling her head back. His lips took possession of hers, demanding and taking until all reservations dissolved along with her will.

Cathe opened, allowing his tongue entrance into her mouth. The feel of being in his arms, his hands in her hair, his lips possessing hers was unbelievably sexy, and she wanted more...but more what? More time in the pillory? More humiliation and confinement? *Not likely.*

She broke off the kiss, sitting up so fast her head bumped his chin. "Please don't do that again." The husky sound of her voice unsettled her.

He had the audacity to laugh. "Don't do what again? Make you burn with desire for me?"

Another gasp escaped, this time along with a few choice words. "The only thing *you* make me is livid, *Lord Asshole*. And you have clearly mistaken disgust for desire."

"That's the second time you have referred to me as such. Does my witch have an ass fetish? I can surely accommodate you on that. As for mistaking your desire for me? I think not." He unexpectedly gripped the hem of her skirt, yanked it up, and cupped her mound before she could stop him.

"You son of a bitch," Cathe seethed, pulling his hand free and jerking her skirt down. The crack of her palm against his face reverberated throughout the trees, sending birds scattering in different directions.

He gripped her wrist in a tight hold and stared down at her with a forced smile. The muscle ticking along his jaw told her he wasn't unaffected by her reprimand. "Do not ever strike me again, witch, or I will take you over my knee in front of the entire castle."

She jerked her arm free, quickly wrapping her hands around the saddle horn. "Just hurry and take me back. I have things to do."

"What things?"

"That's none of your business."

"Everything that takes place on my lands is my business. You would do well to remember that."

* * * *

Bryne had never been more astounded or aroused in all his life. This woman...witch, whatever she was, could rile him faster than anyone he'd ever encountered.

He gazed down at the top of her head in wonder. She spoke to him as if he angered her, and yet her body told a different story. She wanted him...that much he was sure of. He'd seen and felt the evidence of her lust.

What sort of things could she possibly have to do on *his* property? In *his* home? If she thought she would slip around and search for his personal documents, she was in for a rude awakening. Of course he could just let her look. There would be no way in Hades that she would locate them.

"Why did the king send you? Did he think you would learn my secrets by seducing me?"

She blew out an irritated breath. "As I have said before, I have never met your king, nor do

I care to. And I certainly don't know of what secrets you think I am after."

"Why do you refer to His Majesty as *my* king and not *our* king? And you know very well what secrets he sent you after."

"Because he isn't my king. I told you that I came from the twenty-first century and we don't have kings or queens in America. We have presidents."

Though her speech sounded strange and she spoke of treason, Bryne couldn't help but be curious. He wasn't sure if his interest lay more in the treacherous words she spoke or the mind they originated from.

"If you came from the future, what are you doing in 1767, and most importantly, why are you here with me?"

She tilted her face up where he could see her amazing blue eyes. "I told you; I fell asleep reading that book and woke up in your bed. I have no idea why I'm here, only that I need to get back."

Either the woman was crazy or she really was a witch from the future, Bryne decided, gazing at her sincere expression. "If you truly read this book about me, how can you not know of the documents I speak of?"

"I fell asleep about six chapters in. Give me a break." A wrinkle marred her brow. "Wait. I think I remember reading something about a paper you hid."

"I am listening."

"Like I said, I only read a few chapters, but you stashed some important papers in one of the servant's quarters before carving out a stone in your bedroom wall to hide it behind."

His heart began to pound. "You couldn't possibly know that."

"Well, I do. As I've said before, I speak the truth." She paused. "The king offered you the lands in St. Augustine in exchange for the letters your mother left you on her deathbed. Among the correspondences was a document from Frederick, Prince of Wales…your biological father."

"My bio-what?"

"Biological. Your blood father."

He nodded his understanding. "Continue."

"It would seem that Prince Frederick had left specific instructions of what was to become of his illegitimate son upon his death. According to the document, you were to inherit a large sum of gold along with Castle Montabon, the neighboring land bordering your Westminster holding."

Bryne's jaw ached from grinding his teeth. She'd just recited everything in the hidden document. Perhaps she'd read the paper and returned it to its hiding place with intentions of coming back for it later? Unless she really was a witch, he mentally concluded. "Then you are aware of George's order that burned my castle?"

"Yes. I read —"

"And that my wife died shortly after giving birth to our firstborn child?"

"I'm sorry."

"You're sorry? You speak of my past as if you were there, as if you knew me in some way. Everything I owned or had ever known was taken from me in less than a fortnight. Do not pretend to be sorry, Catherine. I much prefer your pride over your pity."

Bryne wasn't sure why he'd verbally attacked the witch. Nothing she'd said made sense, and yet she knew entirely too much about him to allow her to leave.

She quickly turned her face from him, but not before he saw the tears swimming in her eyes. "Catherine?" Lifting his hand, he tucked her hair behind her ear. "Cathe..."

"Will you just take me back now?"

"Why do you cry?" He'd always had a weakness for a woman's tears.

"I am not crying," she barked, stiffening her shoulders. "I'm tired and hungry and I really want some of Betty's simmering stew."

His lips twitched. Attitude, he could handle. "As you wish."

They rode back to the castle in silence with the side of Cathe's sweet bottom pressing against his aching erection. His cock had been hard since the moment he'd stumbled upon her sitting on that seawall with her feet dangling above the water. Truth be told, he'd been hard since the moment he'd found her in his bed. *Damn.*

Chapter Seven

Cathe watched Adair slide from his horse and hold his hands up for her. She gripped his shoulders as he lifted her from the saddle and swept her into his arms once again.

"I can walk on my own," she muttered, settling into the warmth his body offered.

"Horace!" Bryne's voice boomed, nearly deafening her.

A teenage boy instantly burst from the stables, wearing a thin black jacket and pants that were inches too short. "My Lord?"

"See to it that Reaper is taken care of." He handed the kid the reins. "Have him ready to ride in the morning at sunrise. Miss Grier and I will be leaving promptly after breakfast."

"Will the lady be needin' a horse saddled, Sire?"

"No. She will be riding with me."

"Yes, my Lord." Horace bowed and led the stallion toward the stables.

Cathe was once again agitated by the time they reached the castle doors. "Where in the hell are we going at daybreak, and why must I ride with you?"

He ignored her, careening through the giant doors and heading toward the dreaded stairs.

Cathe squeezed her eyes shut and buried her face against his neck. If she were going to spend any length of time in this godforsaken place, she would demand they build some kind of safety railing on the damn stairs.

Why was she thinking in future terms when it came to Adair and his castle of doom? She had no plans of staying here any longer than necessary. The old crone had to be here somewhere, Cathe prayed, gripping Bryne's neck in a tight hold. She just had to find the old lady and demand she send her home.

"Dinner will be ready soon," Bryne announced, barreling into his room. He sat her on the side of his bed and began removing her borrowed shoes.

"I told Betty I would eat with her."

"We do not eat with the help."

That did it. "How dare you!" She snatched her feet from his hold. "We do not eat with the help? Think about how that sounds for a minute. Betty is a human being with feelings and a soul. So are all the other people that work here."

He didn't speak, just watched her as if she had grown another head.

"Look. I realize it's not your fault that you were raised to believe yourself above others, but you have to understand that you're not."

"I'm not what?"

"Above anyone else." Why was she attempting to change a custom in one day that had taken the world centuries to overcome? She blew out a defeated breath. "Forget it."

He suddenly straightened. "I am going to check in with Ansel. I will see you in the dining hall after you have changed. I took the liberty of having some things brought in. I trust that you will find them to your liking." He nodded to an armoire against the far wall before departing the room.

Cathe inched off the bed and curiously advanced toward the armoire, running her fingers over the intricate designs adorning the front. Why was she here? she wondered, pulling the doors open. Not just the year she'd awoken in, but the place...with this particular man?

"Oh, wow." Her breath hitched. Hanging inside were some of the most beautiful dresses Cathe had ever seen. One in particular caught her eye—pale blue in color with an iridescent layer of silk covering the top half of the skirt, giving it a pearl-like appearance.

The smell of fresh pine wafted out as she lifted the dress from the bar it hung from. The hanger itself was made of wood with an iron hook at the top, much like the ones used in the twenty-first century.

"The master sent me to help you, my Lady," a voice announced from behind her.

Cathe spun around in time to see an elderly woman amble into the room holding a tray of ribbons. Her gray hair was swept up under a bright red cap, with a few strands escaping the sides. Her clothing, though faded, appeared neat and clean save for the apron she wore. She'd obviously been cooking.

"Hi." Cathe smiled and extended her hand. "My name's Catherine, but you can call me Cathe."

"Oh, no, my Lady. The master would have my head if I called you by your given name." She gave a quick curtsy. "I'm Wilma."

Cathe let her hand fall away, realizing that history couldn't be altered. Events had already happened that would mold the world into what it was today. No one could change the past—not the book, and certainly not her. But that didn't mean she had to like it. "It's nice to meet you, Wilma."

"Likewise, my Lady."

"Your accent sounds different than Betty's," Cathe pointed out, laying the dress across the foot of the bed.

"I came over from England with the master. Betty was born here." She moved toward the bed. "That's a lovely dress, if I may say so."

Cathe thought so too. "Did you mean that Betty was born in Florida, or that she was born in this castle?"

"Her parents worked for the previous owners, and Lord Adair let her stay on after he took control. He allowed everyone to stay that wanted to."

Cathe filed that away to think on at a later time. "Will you help me with my dress?"

"Oh, yes, my Lady."

"Okay, listen. I'm really uncomfortable with being called my Lady. I am merely an uninvited guest of Lord Adair's. Please, just call me Cathe."

Wilma appeared anxious. She glanced toward the door before meeting Cathe's gaze. "Will you settle for Miss?"

With an inward sigh, Cathe nodded. "Thank you."

The maid beamed and set the tray of ribbons on the dresser. "Turn around, and I'll help you out of your clothes."

"Really, I can undress myself." Cathe reached behind her for the zipper, only to remember the dress laced up the back.

"Nonsense." Wilma brushed her hands aside. "Let me." Within seconds she had the dress undone and pushed off Cathe's shoulders. "There, now step out of it."

Thankful for the shift that Betty had given her, Cathe stepped from the dress and tossed it onto the bed.

Wilma handed her the beautiful baby-blue vision that Cathe had taken from the armoire. "Where is your corset, Miss?"

"I'd rather not wear one, if you don't mind. I tried it on earlier and couldn't breathe."

"But you can't go without it, my Lady. It's not heard of."

Cathe gave her a warm smile. "It's okay, Wilma. I'm only going downstairs. It'll be fine; I promise."

The maid stared at her so long Cathe thought for sure she would argue more. "Put your dress on and give me your back so I can lace you up. Then have a seat on the bench, and I will turn you into Cinderella. Not that it will take much on my part. You are just stunning, Miss."

Heat flushed Cathe's face. She'd never been one to take compliments very well. "Thank you."

Twenty minutes later, Wilma stepped back and clasped her hands in front of her. "Have a look."

Cathe stood and trailed over to a floor mirror in the corner of the room. "Oh, Wilma." Strong emotions washed through her as she took in the reflection staring back at her.

"You're breathtaking." Wilma preened, meeting her gaze in the mirror.

Cathe's long blonde hair was piled loosely atop her head with pale blue ribbons weaving throughout the silky strands, matching her eyes and dress. A touch of pink lined her lips while a dark shade of kohl adorned her eyelids. Even the soft blue shoes were comfortable. But the twenty-something years that had been erased from her face was still the biggest kicker of all.

"How old are you, Miss? If you don't mind me asking."

"Forty seven, as of last week."

Wilma paled. "Did you say forty seven?"

Realizing her mistake, Cathe quickly amended. "Did I say that? I meant twenty...three." How old was she? She had no idea, but she appeared to be somewhere between twenty and twenty-five years old, if her reflection was any indication.

"No matter. You look beautiful, and his Lordship is going to be well pleased."

"We certainly wouldn't want to do anything to displease His Ass-ship, now would we?"

"My Lady!" Wilma gasped, clutching her throat. "We mustn't speak of the master in such a way."

Cathe instantly felt bad. It wasn't Wilma's fault that Cathe had landed in their time, in their castle, anymore than it was Lord Adair's. Then why did he get under her skin so much? "I'm sorry. I shouldn't have said that."

Wilma merely nodded. "Shall we go?"

"Right behind you," Cathe confirmed, following the maid out the bedroom door to the staircase from hell.

Keeping one hand on the wall, Cathe somehow made it to the bottom without falling to her death. She breathed a sigh of relief the moment her foot touched the ground floor.

"Stunning..."

Cathe's heart lurched at the sound of Adair's voice. How could he have such a monumental effect on her? Blanking her expression, she turned to face him. She'd be damned if she would let him see the impact his nearness had on her. "Bryne."

"You are a vision to behold, my Lady." Stepping forward, he held out his arm. "Allow me."

"My Lord?" Wilma questioned, wringing her hands. "Shall I set the table now?"

Bryne sent her a warm smile, telling Cathe that he must be fond of the maid. "That won't be necessary, Wilma. Take the night off. I can handle it from here."

With a quick curtsy and a grateful smile, Wilma hurried from the room, disappearing through an enormous archway off to their left.

Cathe hesitated a second before looping her arm through his. "Where are we going?"

"To dine." The sun had just dipped below the horizon as the two of them made their way outside and down the castle steps. Bryne smiled down at her, and Cathe once again realized how gorgeous his eyes were.

She squinted against the setting sun. "How come you haven't remarried?" Where had that come from? she wondered with more than a little embarrassment.

"You read my fictitious book," he sarcastically replied. "You tell me."

"I didn't get that far. Why not just answer the question?"

He stopped in front of a small wooden door nestled into the side of the castle and turned his body to face hers. "I could ask the same of you, Miss Grier." With a grin, he rapped his knuckles lightly on the door. "You are rapidly on your way to becoming a spinster."

Cathe let the insult roll off her like water off a duck's back. "In my world it's called independence. But you wouldn't know anything about that, would you? Lord Bigot Adair."

A muscle ticked along his jaw. "If you think—"

"My Lord?" Betty interrupted, opening the door with a wooden ladle in hand.

Adair abruptly bowed at the waist. "Do you have room for two more? Miss Grier and I would rather enjoy some stew this evening."

Cathe's mouth fell open in surprise. Betty wasn't unaffected by his words either if the size of her eyes were any indication.

Chapter Eight

"May we come in?" Bryne asked as the maid continued to stand there gawking at him.

"Please, my Lord." She stumbled back, pulling the door wide. "My home is your home."

Covering Cathe's hand with his, he led her over the threshold.

The place was small yet clean. Two neatly made pallets lay in the far right corner of the room, and Bryne made a mental note to have a couple of cots sent over as soon as possible.

A tattered couch sat against the far wall with a wool blanket thrown over it, and a dark green chair sat opposite of it. An old wooden table made up the dining area with four chairs parked underneath and a short bench situated against the wall behind it.

"Something smells wonderful," Bryne remarked, glancing toward a cast-iron pot simmering over an open flame in the fireplace.

"It's beef stew, my Lord." She sent a nervous glance toward Cathe before focusing once again on Bryne. "Can I get ya something to drink, my Lord?" Betty fidgeted, ushering them into the compacted dining area. "Have a seat while I fetch ya some stew."

A knock suddenly sounded, leaving the maid to glance between Adair and the door.

"Go ahead, Betty. We can seat ourselves." Bryne pulled out a chair for Cathe before settling next to her and leaning in close. "You thought I had no civility?"

"It doesn't matter what I think. I won't be here long enough to care."

"But you do care. You're even concerned about what happens to Betty…a servant."

"You say 'servant' like it's a bad thing."

"I do not think they are bad; quite the contrary, which is why I pay them above what is expected."

Several of his men entered the room carrying trays of food—everything from a giant glazed ham to mashed potatoes and green beans. Bryne's stomach promptly growled.

"You pay them? I thought—"

"I know what you thought."

"Sire?" Betty whispered, wringing her hands once again. I ain't complainin', but I don't know why you're here. Have I done somethin' wrong, my Lord?"

"You were kind enough to invite the lovely Miss Grier to dinner this evening, and since I am no longer allowing her out of my sight, I had no choice but to personally extend the invitation to myself as well."

"Oh no, Sire. Your Lordship is always welcome here."

Bryne waved a hand toward the remaining chairs. "Please, have a seat; we are in your home."

Betty slightly paled. "But—"

"The men will serve us tonight. Now, sit. I insist."

Two small boys came barreling through the front door just as Betty settled into her seat. She immediately sprang to her feet, nearly toppling her chair over. "Albert! Joseph! The master's here. Go wash up and wait by your pallets while I make your plates."

Both kids nodded and spun on their dirty, bare heels, heading back the way they came.

Betty returned to her chair. "Sorry about them. They didn't know we was havin' company. They're good boys, I swear."

The maid continued to nervously drone on about her kids, but Bryne wasn't listening. Cathe's sweet scent had drifted up his nose to settle in his cock. He wanted her more than he'd imagined possible. "How old are your lads, Betty?"

"Albert is six, my Lord, and Joseph is five."

Plates of ham, potatoes, and green beans were disbursed among them all by the neatly dressed guards standing at attention behind their master. The pot of stew was set in the center of the table to be dipped into at will.

The food was delicious and the company even better, Bryne silently admitted, watching Cathe openly interact with his maid. The witch was an anomaly to be sure, and he couldn't wait to learn just how much of an aberration she really was.

After finishing their meal with more than a little gusto, the kids darted back outside to enjoy the last remaining hour of play before bath and bedtime.

"Are they always so rambunctious?" Cathe asked with a grin.

"Always, my Lady." Betty returned her smile. "You would make a wonderful mother," the maid pointed out while dipping another bowl of stew. "How many children do ya plan on havin', if ya don't mind me askin'?"

Something shifted in Cathe's gaze seconds before she abruptly stood. "Will you excuse me, please? I need to use the restroom. I mean the lavatory."

Bryne stood also. "Are you not feeling well? I will escort you back to my room."

"I'm fine. I'll just use the one I saw on the way here."

"In the courtyard, Catherine? That's for the servants and soldiers, not for—"

"Don't say it," Cathe interrupted. "I'll be back in a few minutes. Enjoy your meal." With that, she rushed out.

Bryne had yet to see her react in such a way. He went back over Betty's comment in his mind, but nothing the maid said should have upset Cathe so. He reluctantly sat and continued with his meal. "Your stew is divine, Betty. You should be working in the kitchens."

"Did I say somethin to hurt Miss Grier, Sire? Me and my big mouth. I'm always talkin' without thinkin'."

"I'm sure it was nothing you said." He patted her hand and changed the subject. "What happened to your children's father?"

"He died of the pox when Joseph was still in the womb."

"I am sorry to hear that." Bryne would raise her earnings first thing in the morning.

The door opened, and the maid's youngest son ran inside before skidding to a stop next to Bryne's chair. The kid's lower lip quivered as he stared up at Adair with huge eyes. "Him hurt her."

"What did you just say?" Bryne's heart lurched. Surely he'd heard the boy wrong.

"Him's hittin' her," Joseph repeated before bursting into tears.

Bryne's sword was in hand before his chair finished toppling over behind him.

The sprint through the courtyard was an eternity for Adair as he stormed toward the lavatory as fast as his legs would carry him. The door standing ajar told him what he dreaded most. Cathe was gone.

"Cathe!" he shouted, scanning the darkness in search of some kind of movement— anything that would lead him to her.

Doors were suddenly thrown open and dozens of servants rushed outside with swords drawn.

"Catherine Grier has been taken," Bryne bellowed, heading toward the stables. "I need every available man mounted and ready to go. I want her found immediately. Now, move."

"Yes, Sire," they chorused, scattering to do his bidding.

Who could have done this? Adair seethed as he entered the livery and raced to Reaper's stall. Bryne would choke the life from the man with his bare hands when he found him. And he would find him, no matter how long it took.

"Over here, my Lord," a soldier called out from near the well in the center of the courtyard.

Bryne released the latch on the stall door and sped back the way he'd come, not stopping until he reached the castle's well. There, lying facedown on the ground was his beautiful witch.

He dropped to his knees beside her and gently rolled her over. Dirt and grass mixed with blood were smeared along the side of her face. Rage poured through him with a force that was staggering.

"Virgil?" he growled, gently lifting Cathe's limp body into his arms. He stood, turning to face his second-in-command. He knew Haskell was near without needing a visual. The man had always been there when Bryne needed him.

"Sire?" Haskell stepped forward, fully dressed, his hand resting on the hilt of his sword.

Always at the ready, Bryne silently acknowledged. "Take as many men as you need and scour the surrounding area. The ones left are to search the grounds. I want no stone left unturned."

Haskell briefly clasped Adair's shoulder before striding briskly toward the stables, barking orders as he went.

"Ansel?" Bryne shouted on his way to the castle doors.

"Yes, my Lord?"

"Send the doctor to my room. Have him hurry. Miss Grier has been hurt."

"Doctor Peadmire ain't here, my Lord. He's deliverin' a baby over at the Bickford's place. Left early this morning."

Bryne burst through the castle doors, taking the stairs two at a time to the second floor with Ansel tight on his heels. "Ansel?"

"Sire?"

Get me some warm water, a washcloth, a towel, and some bandages. Be quick about it," Bryne ordered, entering his bedroom. He unsheathed his sword and propped it against the headboard within easy reach.

"Yes, my Lord," the servant responded in a high-pitched voice before spinning around and scurrying back toward the stairs.

Bryne laid Cathe's limp body in the center of his bed and adjusted the oil lamp on the bedside table, flooding the room with light.

"Cathe, can you hear me?" He gently touched the uninjured side of her face. "You're going to be fine. I will find the man that did this and make him pay. I vow it."

Her pink lips slightly parted, and a soft moan escaped. "Bryne…"

"I'm here, love. Can you tell me where all you're injured?"

She reached up and touched the side of her head, wincing as she probed near an angry-looking lump near her hairline with blood seeping from it.

Bryne found it difficult to control his rage, knowing that someone had dared to touch her, to harm her in any way. He prayed the guy didn't run, thereby robbing Bryne of the pleasure of torturing him slowly.

"Easy now. Ansel will be back shortly with bandages. I'll have you fixed up in no time." He gently brushed her hair from her face. "Did he touch— Are you—" Taking a deep breath, he tried again. "Were you hurt anywhere else?"

Relief poured through him when she shook her head. He was never allowing her from his sight again. She could have been forced, stabbed, or killed if Betty's son hadn't happened along and run for help.

Ansel returned with an armload of supplies. "Where shall I put these, my Lord?"

Bryne nodded toward the bedside table. "That will be all, Ansel. Thank you."

"Just tug the cord if you need me, Sire." After emptying his arms of their burden, Ansel left the room, pulling the door closed behind him.

Dipping a cloth into the warm water, Bryne set out to cleanse Cathe's wound, wiping the blood and dirt from her face as gently as possible. "You're very fortunate, Miss Grier. A little lower and—"

"I could have been killed," she finished for him. "So, now it's Miss Grier?"

Adair paused, his gaze dropping to her striking blue eyes only to find them open and staring back at him. His heartbeat picked up its pace the longer he studied her guileless expression. He could lose himself in those eyes, and that scared him more than the thought of her being attacked. "You prefer witch then?"

"I think the question is, do *you* prefer witch?"

Was she watching his mouth? He slowly lowered his head. "I prefer you, Catherine Grier, witch or not, as long as you're alive and here with me."

"But what if—"

His lips covered hers, cutting off any doubts she was about to voice. He didn't want her doubts, uncertainties, or any other negative thoughts she might have. No, he only wanted her—Catherine, the witch—bared to him, open to him and coming for him.

Surrender had never tasted so good, he thought as she sighed into his mouth, her body going lax beneath him. Nor had it ever felt so right...

Chapter Nine

Cathe's entire body was on fire. It wasn't that she'd never been with a man before, but the few she'd had experience with paled in comparison to Bryne Adair, from the gentle way his lips moved over hers to the feel of his hands in her hair.

It made no sense, and maybe it was wrong in some way, but God help her, she wanted him, wanted him touching her and loving her. But most of all, she wanted him to make her feel alive—something she hadn't felt since Craig.

He broke off the kiss and dragged his lips across her jaw to her ear. "Feel me, Catherine. The real me. Not the lord or the asshole you think I am, but the man, the man that needs you right now, this moment in time, more than breath."

All doubt dissipated with Adair's vulnerable declaration. It didn't matter that she had to return home or that she couldn't take him with her when she did. No one was promised tomorrow. She'd found that out the hard way when the love of her life and unborn child had been taken from her all those years ago. "Yes."

He lifted his head, brushing his lips across hers once again. "Are you sure?"

The door suddenly crashing against the wall cut off any response she was about to give.

"Give me one reason why I should not lop off your insufferable head," Bryne snarled, jumping from the bed and wrapping his fingers around Ansel's throat.

"The king and his army are nigh, my Lord," the servant wheezed, his beady eyes bulging.

Adair released him but didn't step back. "How far out are they?"

"Less than a mile, Sire. Ya must make haste."

"I run from no man," Bryne growled, going for the servant's throat once again.

Cathe almost felt sorry for the servant. Almost. He did, after all, leave her to freeze to death in the courtyard pillory.

Ansel's bulging gaze briefly swung in her direction before settling on his master once again. "It ain't you he comes for, my Lord. It's the witch."

"What does he want with me?" Cathe threw her legs over the side of the bed, immediately regretting it. Dizziness assaulted her and nausea rolled through her stomach.

"It makes perfect sense," Bryne answered for Ansel, taking a step back. He slowly turned to face Cathe. "He has come to retrieve his property."

Pain settled inside her heart to replace her earlier euphoria. "I'm not his property. I've told you before; I have never met the man. Why won't you believe me?"

"Ansel?"

"Sire?"

"See that she doesn't leave this room."

"Yes, my Lord."

Snatching up his sword, Adair stormed out without a backward glance, leaving Cathe alone with Ansel once again.

"He ain't gonna be able to save ya, ya know," the servant taunted, sauntering closer.

Something in the guy's eyes set off warning bells inside her brain. "Save me from what?" Her gaze scanned the room for something, anything that she could use as a weapon.

"From this." He tugged a dagger from his boot, continuing toward her with an eerie look on his face.

Cathe scrambled across the bed, jumping to her feet on the other side. "What did I ever do to you?"

Ansel smiled, revealing rotted teeth. "It ain't what ya did; it's what ya can do. Witches are worth a pretty penny in these parts."

"You're planning on selling me?" She couldn't believe what she was hearing.

"I done sold ya to the king, and now he's come for ya." Ansel laughed—an ugly, unnatural sound that gave Cathe the creeps.

"You will never get away with this. I'll tell Lord Adair what you've done, and he'll rip your head off."

"Ya think he'll believe a witch over a trusty servant?" Ansel skirted the bed, stalking her into a corner.

"I'll scream," Cathe threatened, backing against the wall.

"No one will hear ya," he sneered, twisting the dagger handle in his hand.

A muffled *thump*, and the sight of his body dropping at her feet brought her out of her terrorized state.

"Are ya all right, my Lady?"

"Betty? Thank God!" Cathe cried, wrapping the maid in a hug.

"We must hurry, Miss. I don't know how long he'll be out," Betty whispered, pulling back and tucking a bloodied rock into the pocket of her skirt. She grabbed onto Cathe's hand. "Come on."

A million things skated through Cathe's mind as she ran as close to Betty as possible. The maid paused at the stairs and glanced over the side before pulling Cathe along down the steep flight.

They didn't stop until they reached the bottom, entering Ansel's room undetected. Betty closed the door behind them and leaned against it. "We ain't got much time, Miss, so listen good. There's an underground tunnel just beyond that fireplace." She pointed toward the back of the room. "Run to the end of it and wait for me. I'll be along shortly with a horse. Now move before ya get caught."

Cathe's heart pounded hard enough she thought she could see it pumping through her dress. "How did you know about Ansel?"

"My boy told me who hit ya."

Thank God for Betty and her son, Cathe thought, staring into her newfound friend's eyes. "Where will I go? I don't know anyone here."

"Ride east for about a mile until you come to a cabin sittin' next to a cornfield. That's my brother's place. His name's Ellis. Tell him I sent ya. I'll check on ya as soon as it's safe."

"What if I run into the king and his soldiers?"

"Ya won't. They come from the north. Hurry! Ya ain't got much time." Betty opened the door and left without another word.

Cathe's legs threatened to buckle beneath her. How the hell she had gotten herself into this mess was beyond her. She darted across the room to find her escape route.

A narrow, wooden door was situated to the right of the fireplace. She gripped the handle and pulled it open. *Oh, hell no.*

Cobwebs hung across the opening, blowing in a nonexistent breeze that could be seen but not felt. "I hate spiders, I hate spiders, I hate spiders," she chanted, brushing the webs aside to enter the dark portal.

If there were two things in the world that Cathe had a problem with besides running for her life, it was claustrophobia and arachnophobia.

"Son of a bitch," she whispered, stepping into the tunnel and pulling the door shut behind her, casting the underground shaft in total darkness. If she got out of this alive, she would hunt Ansel down and lock him in the pillory naked and drop a beehive next to his feet.

Keeping her hands out in front of her, she stumbled along for what seemed an eternity until a small sliver of light ahead sent relief pouring through her in great waves of gratitude.

She crept to the crack and peeked out into the daylight beyond. Her breath continued to come in rapid bursts, echoing off the walls of the tunnel to drown out the ringing in her ears.

"Miss," Betty abruptly called in a hushed tone. "Are ya here, Miss?"

Cathe could hear the rustling of bushes before easing the door open and glancing around. "Is it safe to come out?"

"Yes, Miss, but ya must make haste."

"Where are we?" They were definitely outside the castle walls.

"This is the only unknown passage into the castle. It's kept hidden and is always guarded from the top of the wall there." She jerked her chin upward.

"I'm assuming it's Ansel's job to guard the wall."

"Yes, Miss." The maid backed up a step and waved her arm out to the side. "Here's a horse. I packed ya enough supplies for a few days. Ellis will make sure that ya have plenty to see ya through until I can figure out how to get ya out of this mess."

"Why are you helping me?"

"You was good to me when most weren't. Now climb up there and don't stop till ya see the cornfields."

Cathe threw her arms around the woman and hugged her tight. "Thank you, Betty. I won't forget you for this." She mounted the horse before she changed her mind and crawled back inside the spider cave.

Betty slapped the horse's rear, leaving Cathe no choice but to ride or fall.

* * * *

Bryne Adair pulled up on his reins and lifted his arm for his men to follow suit as he waited to be addressed by his king.

"How fare thee, Adair?" George greeted from behind a wall of soldiers.

"I am well. I trust that I have found you to be prosperous?" Bryne watched as George's horse ambled to the front line with the slightest knee command.

"Prosperous indeed." His gaze scanned the army of men behind Adair.

Bryne being more of a get-to-the-point person…did exactly that. "If you have come to accompany me to the meeting with Governor Grant on the morrow, I do not see or feel the need for an escort, Sire."

George's face turned red. "You dare to speak to your king in such a manner?"

"You dare to enter my lands under false pretenses with the intention of taking what belongs to me?" Bryne shot back, rage boiling beneath the surface.

"Stand down before I have you hanged."

Bryne would die before allowing George to get his pompous hands on Catherine. Then again, he may have already had his hands on her, Bryne's mind whispered. The thought of that arrogant bastard touching her enraged him.

A horse came galloping to the front line, carrying one of Bryne's men. "A word, my Lord?"

With a nod, Bryne broke away from the group, stopping just out of hearing range. "What brings you here?"

"She's gone, Sire," the guard panted, glancing toward the king and his men.

Bryne saw red. "What do you mean she's gone?"

"Wilma sent Doctor Peadmire to have a look at her upon his return. He found Ansel on the floor with a whopping knot on the back of his head, but no sign of the woman, Sire."

"I want every available man out looking for her. She couldn't have gotten far on foot."

"Yes, my Lord." The guard swung his horse around and sped back toward the castle, kicking up dust in his wake.

Bryne returned to the front line and faced his king. "It would appear that you have wasted a trip, Your Majesty. Now, if you will excuse me, I have something quite urgent to attend to."

George broke away from his soldiers, signaling for Bryne to follow. They stopped outside of hearing distance. "I do not know what you think to gain by hiding the witch or the documents. Think of what would happen to your sister and her children if it were known that her brother protected a witch."

The unveiled threat to his family wasn't lost on Bryne. It took an enormous amount of effort to keep his sword in its sheath. "Think of the scandal to your family if the throne were to receive word of our father's dying wish for his illegitimate son."

"You wouldn't dare."

Bryne kept his face blank. "I'm sure that Governor Grant will understand my absence on the morrow as I tend this pressing matter, Your Majesty. Please give my apologies."

The obvious threat infuriated George, if the purple hue of his face was any indication. "Retreat," the king ordered without taking his gaze from Adair. "It would appear that our services are no longer needed," he bit out, turning to go.

"Perhaps another time, brother," Bryne taunted, bowing his head.

"Count on it."

Adair waited for the last of the king's men to disappear over the rise, gripped his reins, and turned his horse back toward home. He glanced over at his second-in-command riding close by his side. "We have to find her, Virgil. She has no idea what dangers lie in wait out there."

"I will not rest until she is found, my Lord. You have my word." Virgil shifted in his saddle. "How did you manage to keep George from the castle?"

"He is unsure of how far he can push me. And besides, with all his arrogance, he does not want to see me dead."

"You must have good reason to believe this."

Bryne thought of the documents safely tucked away inside his castle walls. "I do." He changed the subject. "It will be dark soon, Haskell. The Mocama—"

"The likelihood of her encountering a native in this area is highly unlikely, Sire. Rest easy, old man. We will find her."

"Thank you, Virgil. And for the thousandth time, it's Bryne."

Haskell only smiled and spurred his horse into a gallop, leaving Bryne to catch up.

Chapter Ten

The sun was beginning to set as Cathe arrived at the top of a hill looking down on the biggest cornfield she had ever seen. Trees were scattered along the right side of the property while corn covered the left for what seemed like miles.

A small cabin situated between the two could barely be seen for the dense canopy of trees it rested beneath. Smoke from a chimney swirled its way through the foliage to dissolve in the chilly February air.

Cathe froze as a low voice sounded from close behind her. "Who are you?"

"My name is Catherine Grier."

"State your business."

"I need your help."

The owner of the voice stepped up next to her horse, pointing a rifle in her direction. "What makes you think I would help you?"

The guy was a handsome young man with light-colored hair and hazel eyes. He looked to be about six feet tall, but she couldn't be sure from her position on the horse. "Are you Ellis?"

The rifle wavered slightly. "Do I know you?"

"No, but your sister does. Betty sent me. She said that you would assist me with a place to hide for a while."

He lowered the weapon, a crease marring his brow. "Who are you hiding from, if you don't mind me asking?"

"Lord Adair."

"Lord...? Have you lost your mind, woman? Do you know what he will do to me if he finds you here?"

"I wouldn't dream of putting you in a dangerous position. Betty said you could help me with supplies and point me in a safe direction."

"Yeah, well, Betty has lost her mind." He ran a hand through his sandy-blond hair. "Come on. We must make haste if we are to stay ahead of Lord Adair. He's a crafty one."

Relief was swift. "Thank you, Ellis."

Cathe directed her horse to follow the young man down the hill to his cabin. The place was even more beautiful up close. "Is this all yours?"

"It was deeded to me in exchange for the crops I provide along with any legal assistance that may be required."

Surprised, Cathe gaped at the man's back. "You're an attorney?"

He glanced back with a smile. "I have studied law since I was able to read."

No wonder his speech sounded different than his sister's, she thought with more than a little pride for the guy. "How much longer until you receive your law degree?"

"My what?"

They don't have law degrees yet because law school wasn't available until the late 1700's and uncommon still until the early twentieth century. "Oh, nothing. Just something I heard somewhere."

They arrived at the cabin, and Ellis helped her to dismount.

"Something smells wonderful," Cathe proclaimed, studying her surroundings.

"It's a pot roast and biscuits, my Lady. Would you like to eat before we go?"

"Please call me Cathe. And I would love to, but I have no idea how much time I have. May I take some with me?"

"Absolutely." A blush crept up his neck. "Do you need to… I mean…would you like to freshen up while I gather your supplies, Miss?"

She hadn't had a bath since the one she'd been forced to take with Adair. A vision of his godlike body floated through her mind, leaving her weak in the knees. "I would love to freshen up. Thank you, Ellis."

Cathe preceded him inside the clean, cozy cabin. The guy had no idea how retro this would be two hundred and fifty years in the future.

"Everything you need should be in there." He waved his hand toward a room in the back. "Give a yell if you need anything."

Twenty minutes later, Cathe emerged from the cabin and once again mounted her horse. The biscuit she'd eaten had helped to take the edge off her hunger, but man, she could almost feel her stomach eating her backbone. "Where are we going?"

Ellis climbed onto his horse and turned toward the tree line. "To a place where Betty and I grew up." He glanced over at Cathe. "The property changed hands several years ago, but the last man that purchased it died shortly after he moved in. It's been vacant ever since. You'll be temporarily safe there until you can decide on what you're going to do."

Cathe let that sink in. "Aren't you curious as to why I'm running from Adair?"

"Of course I am, but I figure if you wanted me to know, you would tell me."

"I'll keep that in mind," she returned, staying close behind him as they trekked through the woods.

"Once we break from the trees we will follow the shoreline. The property is just a few miles up the coast."

"Sounds good."

The two of them rode in silence for most of the trip along the coastline. At any other time, Cathe would have appreciated the beauty of the land, but not today. Her thoughts were centered on a giant pain in her ass. *Adair*.

Why couldn't she stop thinking about him? He was an overbearing thorn in her side that she was better off without. He treated people as if they were beneath him in some way. Hell, he'd even tossed her into a room with Ansel her first night in the castle. He'd forced her to bathe with him and had thrown her over his shoulder like a sack of feed while he put his hands on her rear. He was an asshole, plain and simple.

She supposed he did have a few good qualities like stocking the armoire with all those beautiful dresses for her and taking her to Betty's to eat even though it was frowned upon by those of his station.

The way he'd looked at her with those gunmetal-gray eyes, his lips on hers, taking, possessing, and the feel of his hands on her body had nearly driven her crazy… Drove her crazy still.

"We're here," Ellis announced, dismounting and tethering his horse to a low-hanging branch.

Cathe shook off her thoughts to take in her surroundings. The small house in front of her was in desperate need of help. One of the windows had been busted out, and a gaping hole made up the top left corner of the roof. Knee-high weeds surrounded the place in a cocoon of spiders and snakes with an obvious side of rats.

A shiver ran through her. "Will you do a critter check for me?"

Ellis laughed, holding up his arms to help her down from her horse. "I'll do one better. How about you gather some firewood while I make the place presentable?"

"Sounds like a plan," she agreed, remembering some driftwood she'd spotted on the beach. "I'll be back in a flash."

* * * *

"It grows too dark to see, Sire," Haskell unnecessarily pointed out. "Shall we make camp for the night?"

"We'll set up under that thicket over there," Bryne reluctantly conceded. "But we leave at first light."

"If not for the late start, we would have found her by now."

Bryne ground his teeth, well aware his second-in-command spoke the truth. "I had no inkling His Majesty would arrive today anymore than I knew Ansel couldn't be trusted."

Haskell threw his leg over the side of the horse and dropped lithely onto his feet. "How can you be sure Ansel betrayed you, Sire? You mentioned the king's previous knowledge of the witch. How is Ansel at fault?"

"You're going to continue not using my name, aren't you?"

"Aye, my Lord. Now what of Ansel?"

Bryne dismounted and went about helping Haskell with setting up camp. "No other knew of George's approach. Ansel sounded the alarm of the king's presence on my lands, and he claims the witch overtook him and escaped."

"You are sure that she did not?"

"Ansel's dagger was on the floor when Doctor Peadmire discovered him, and yet there was a lump on the back of his head."

"Ah, I see. How could the witch have gotten a rock, slipped around behind him, and hit him over the head while being held at knifepoint."

"My point exactly, Virgil. She couldn't have. But someone did, and I intend to find out whom."

Haskell nodded. "It could have been anyone, Sire. She's a comely little thing with her golden hair and eyes that rival the sky."

Bryne had Virgil on the ground with his forearm against his friend's neck before he realized what had happened. "She is mine. Friends or no, you touch her and I will remove your head."

"Easy, old man." Virgil grinned. "One might think you have feelings for the lady."

Jumping to his feet, Bryne brushed off his pants, held out his hand for Virgil, and pulled him up. "Get a fire started while I unload the horses."

What had gotten into him? He'd just attacked his closest friend in a fit of jealousy over a witch claiming to be from the future.

Bryne glanced over at Haskell who was now gathering nearby twigs for the fire. It was no secret that women found Bryne's second-in-command desirable and even went so far as to fight for his affection. What if Cathe found him appealing as well?

"Your witch has no interest in me."

"Am I that obvious?" Bryne collected food and blankets from the horses while his second-in-command started the fire.

Virgil laughed. "Understandably so, my Lord. She is a prize to be sure, but her interests lay solely in you, Sire. If you cannot see that, perhaps you should open your eyes, for it is beyond transparent to the rest of us."

"Us?"

Virgil turned away, but not before Bryne noticed the color staining his face. "Just some of the staff and me. We have a wager on how long it will take for you to propose."

Bryne's stomach twisted. He couldn't propose to a witch, much less an addled witch who thought she could travel through time.

He pasted on a smile that he didn't feel. "I trust you didn't shell out too much coin, Haskell. I would certainly hate to see you lose over my lack of wedding intentions."

"We shall see, my Lord. We shall see."

* * * *

Awakening long before daylight, Bryne folded his sleeping gear and packed up his horse. "I think we should circle back around and check the east side before hitting the coastline."

Virgil followed Adair's lead and mounted his own horse. "Why would she head into the forest when the water is so close? There would be far less chances of running into undesirables along the coast."

Those undesirables were the reason Bryne's heart hadn't stopped racing since Catherine's escape. *If she happens to stumble upon one...* He couldn't finish the thought.

"Most likely because she figures that is exactly what we would do. No, I think she would stay to the trees."

Two hours later, they were skirting the cornfield that bordered Ellis Burland's place. "Whatever happened to Burland's family, my Lord?"

"His father died in the war fifteen years ago. I'm not sure about the mother, but his sister Betty has been employed by me since I moved into the castle a few years ago."

"It was good that you leased the young man this place. He's a hard-working sort."

"Indeed he is," Bryne agreed. "He keeps my tax logs and supplies me with any other legal provisions I might require also."

"Let's not forget the corn."

"Where are you going with this?"

"Just stating the obvious, my Lord. He no doubt has friends in high places, not to mention I'm sure he is friendly with the natives. Who better to help someone disappear than a baby-face lawyer with dashing good looks and a pocket full of coin?"

Adair kicked his horse into a gallop, suddenly eager to reach Burland's cabin. Haskell was right about Ellis Burland. He was a big, strong, handsome fellow with enough money to make a female happy, including Bryne's Catherine.

"Was it something I said, Sire?" Haskell grinned, stopping his horse next to Adair's.

Bryne ignored the jab. "You take the back; I'm going in the front. If you find him, do not alert him to our intensions. I want to speak with him first."

With a quick nod, Haskell steered his stallion toward the rear of the cabin.

Adair dropped to the ground and sauntered through the front yard to the porch. "Ellis?" he called out, rapping his knuckles on the door. When no answer came, he let himself inside.

The place was exceptionally clean, and the smell of food permeated the air, telling Bryne that Ellis hadn't long been gone.

"Something smells delicious in here. Think he would mind if we helped ourselves?" Haskell asked, entering the backdoor. "His horse isn't here. Two sets of tracks leading toward the tree line. Think she's with him?"

A thought occurred to Bryne. "Ellis is Betty's brother. My guess is she helped Cathe escape and sent her here." He spun toward the door.

"I take it you know where they went?" Virgil questioned, jogging to keep up.

Bryne mounted his horse. "If my instincts are correct, we should catch up to them in a matter of hours."

Chapter Eleven

"I'll come back in a few days to bring you more supplies, Miss Grier. Try not to stray too far from the beach; wild animals lurk in the woods."

"Thank you so much for everything, Ellis. I'll never be able to repay you enough."

"Don't mention it. Here, take this." He freed a dagger from a leather sheath attached to his belt. "You'll need it more than me."

She accepted the knife and wrapped her savior in a hug. "Thank you again, and be safe going home."

"Take care, Miss." He pulled back with a blush staining his cheeks and mounted his horse. With a wave, he spurred the black Arabian into a run.

Cathe stared after Ellis's retreating back until he disappeared from her sight. Anxiety tightened her gut at the reality of her situation. She was completely alone in the wrong time and place. Nothing made sense anymore; not the reasons for her being here and certainly not the unusual attraction she felt for Adair.

She ran a hand down her face and drifted back inside the house. The first thing she needed to do was figure out how to find the old crone responsible for her situation to start with and demand she send her home.

Most of the previous night had been spent cleaning the house with Ellis and gathering firewood, which meant that Cathe now had time to do other things such as eat and plan.

Stoking the fire in the wood-burning stove, she grabbed the fishing pole that Ellis had fashioned for her, picked up the sack of worms he'd gathered, and traipsed down to the water's edge.

Cathe had grown up fishing with her dad on weekends, which made her somewhat of a pro, she told herself while twisting her hair into a knot. If she had to live out here for God knew how long until she could return home, at least she wouldn't starve.

Thirty minutes and three catfish later, Cathe trudged her way back to the house with her soon-to-be meal. She couldn't remember ever being so hungry or having such a full bladder.

After using the old-fashioned chamber pot, she emptied it, rinsed it in the river, and went about making breakfast.

"That had to be the best-tasting fish I've ever had," she said aloud while washing her used dishes and covering her leftovers to eat later.

Grabbing her bag and the dagger that Ellis had given her, she struck out for the river once again. Going from two showers a day to bathing in the river was not something she wanted to get used to, but it would have to do until she could get back to twenty-first-century civilization.

"Damn it." Cathe sighed. She'd forgotten that the dress laced up the back. With angry movements, she picked up the dagger, gripped the hem of the dress, and cut it straight up the front before stepping out of it. With any luck, she'd be able to fashion a comfortable outfit from it.

She removed the shift next, picked up the cake of soap, and rushed into the water before she changed her mind and took a military bath from a bowl.

The icy bite of the water stole her breath but didn't stop her from diving in. Lathering up, she dunked once more in an attempt to rinse as much soap from her hair as possible.

Her teeth were chattering as she broke the surface and pushed her hair back from her face.

"You prefer pneumonia over being with me?"

Cathe's heart turned over, and she slammed her arms over her chest. "How long have you been standing there?"

"Your body is perfection, my beautiful witch, but even that will not save you from my wrath."

"How did you find me?" she managed to ask through the chattering of her teeth.

"Come out before you freeze to death."

"Turn around."

One of Bryne's eyebrows lifted. "I will not."

"Then I'll stay right here."

With an exasperated sigh, he gave her his back, mumbling something about witches or women—she couldn't be sure.

Cathe hurried from the water as fast as her shivering legs would carry her. She snatched up her towel and wrapped it around her body before gathering her belongings and stuffing them into the bag. "Okay, it's safe."

Bryne turned and scooped her up into his arms, ignoring her gasp of outrage.

"Put me down," she demanded while snuggling deeper into his warmth.

"Methinks you are a bossy bit of witch goods." He strolled back to the house, marched inside, and set her on her feet in front of the still-warm stove. "You have some explaining to do."

The door opened and Virgil poked his head inside. "Shall I make camp, my Lord, or journey back before it grows late?"

Adair quickly moved his body between Cathe and Haskell, effectively cutting off the guy's view of her partial nudity. "I would prefer that you be there to keep an eye on the king in the event he changes his mind and decides to molest my castle in my absence. Miss Grier and I have some unfinished business. I am not certain when I will return and would appreciate your discretion of my whereabouts."

"Always, my Lord." Virgil closed the door, leaving Cathe alone with a very determined Lord Bryne Adair.

* * * *

"He's after me, isn't he?"

The tremor in Cathe's voice could mean one of two things. She either feared the king would hunt her down, or she feared that he wouldn't.

Bryne turned to face her. "Why would you think it is you His Majesty wants?"

She adjusted the towel more tightly around her, hooking it under her arm. "Because Ansel sold me to him."

"How can you be sure?"

"Ansel admitted it to me right before he tried stabbing me in the heart."

Pure, unadulterated rage clawed its way through Adair's body, slowly wrapping him in a web of fury that threatened to snap his notorious control.

He had to force his teeth apart to speak again. "I am sorry for putting you in that position, Catherine. You may rest assured he will not live to see the sun rise in the morning."

Her eyes grew round. "You're going to kill him?"

Bryne ignored her question and stalked to the door. He jerked it open in time to find Virgil readying to leave. "One more thing, Haskell."

"Sire?"

"Ansel dies before your horse is stabled for the night."

Other than a slight eye squint, Virgil showed no outward emotion to Bryne's demand. "Hanged, my Lord?"

"Aye. I want him made an example of."

"I'll see to, Sire."

"Thank you, my friend."

Bryne shut the door and trailed back toward the stove where Cathe stood shivering.

Water droplets from her hair dripped onto her bare shoulders to trickle down her chest and disappear beneath the towel.

Blood rushed to his cock on cue. He wanted her so much that his body ached with the effort of holding back. "I don't know how much longer I can keep my hands off you, witch. It's tormenting me to stand here looking at you."

"Then don't look."

"Did Ellis touch you?" he growled, taking a step closer to her.

"That's none of your business," she shot back, lifting her chin with the slightest show of arrogance that turned him on even more.

He grabbed her wrist and jerked her flush against his body. "I am going to ask you once more. Did Burland put his hands on you?"

"No. He was a perfect gentleman, which is more than I can say for you," she snapped, twisting to get free.

Bryne only held on tighter. "You think I'm not a gentleman?" Leaning down, he brushed her neck with his lips. "If I were not honorable, I would have your nude form splayed out before me, your thighs open, and my tongue licking the honey from your sweet peach until you begged me to stop."

Her soft intake of breath and subtle body movements weren't lost on him. He softly growled in her ear. "Would you like that, beautiful Catherine? To come on my face while I lick you to release? Or I could bury my cock inside you slow and easy until you plead for me to take you hard and fast."

He took a deep breath. "I want you, Catherine Grier, witch and seductress. Let me have you."

* * * *

Cathe's entire body felt liquid. Her arms had gone limp and her legs were threatening to buckle. Desire like nothing she'd ever known coursed through her veins, heating her from the inside out.

The feel of Bryne's rock-hard erection pressing against her stomach drove her insane with need. She'd never experienced this level of attraction, and she wanted him just as much as he wanted her…if not more.

She'd likely return home soon, and with that, her life would go back the way it was before this maddening ride through time. She might never get the chance to feel this mind-altering desire again. "Yes. God, yes."

Bryne instantly swept her into his arms and spun in a half circle as if deciding where to take her.

"In there," Cathe breathed, the husky sound of her voice obvious even to her.

He strode toward the door she'd indicated, shouldering his way through, nearly taking it off its hinges in his haste. The mattress Ellis had taken out and dusted for her lay on the floor covered in tattered blankets next to a broken bed frame.

Depositing her onto her back, Bryne swiftly discarded her towel and straightened to remove his own clothes.

Cathe couldn't take her gaze from his exposed chest as he tossed his shirt to the side and unlaced the front of his pants.

"I need you to be sure, Cathe. Once I touch you, I will not be able to stop."

She'd been wet and swollen with need since his heated admission by that stove. "I'm sure."

Cathe watched in fascination as he toed off his boots, gripped the waistband of his pants, and pulled them down his legs before stepping out of them.

He straightened, allowing her a minute to take in his masculine form. Her gaze devoured his massive chest, following the hairline down his stomach to his overly endowed, engorged cock. "I've never seen a man as beautiful as you."

"I do not want to think of you knowing other men, beautiful or not."

His possessiveness should have angered her, but it didn't. If anything, it made her want him even more. "That was a compliment."

He knelt next to her on the mattress and ran his fingertips lightly up her leg. "You are beyond magnificent. Not just your beauty, but your strange words, your bravery, your outrageous thoughts. You beguile me, my temptress from another time, and I fear I cannot let you go."

Cathe's heart flipped with his touching confession. Whether from fear or desire, she wasn't sure. Perhaps it was both, she silently admitted to herself.

"No tears. I will not harm you."

"I..." Cathe wasn't aware she'd been crying. She stared up into Bryne's gorgeous face, trying to call up a vision of Craig, but nothing appeared. For the first time since his death all those years ago, she couldn't remember what he looked like.

Bryne lifted her leg closest to him and settled between her open thighs. "So sexy," he growled, lowering his head and nuzzling her breasts. He slowly ran his tongue over one before sucking a pebbled tip into his mouth.

Cathe gripped the back of his head, writing beneath him with every strong pull on her oversensitive nipple. Mindless moans escaped her as he moved to the next one to lavish it with the same erotic attention he'd given the other.

Moisture flooded her thighs as he continued his unending torture of her breasts. He abruptly lowered his body, aligning his thick erection with her soft mound and flexed his hips, effectively pressing the underside of his cock against her swollen clit.

Cathe cried out in pleasure, thrashing her head from side to side as he continued to suck her nipple deep and grind against her achingly sensitive pussy. "Oh, God, Bryne please. I can't take it."

Her nipple suddenly popped free of his mouth. He dragged his tongue up her neck and nudged her face to the side before taking hold of her hands and bringing them over her head, all the while his hips continued their torment. "Come for me."

A gasp burst from her as he applied more pressure to her clit. "I can't. I want you inside me."

"Yes, you can," he insisted, continuing to grind against her. "I'm a big man, Cathe; a big man that's going to fuck you hard. I need to be sure you're ready to take me...all of me." He jerked her arms up higher and rocked more firmly against her. "Come for me. Now."

Her back arched as spasms instantly rocked her from head to feet. Wave after wave of pleasure coursed through her abdomen, centered on the incredible friction against her clit.

"Yes. Just like that, my beautiful witch." He groaned, pressing the head of his cock against her opening.

Cathe's eyes rolled back with the feel of him pushing inside her. The pressure, the stretching, the pleasure was more than she'd thought it would be.

"Open for me," he growled, thrusting deeper. "You can take me."

Another orgasm built as he plunged into her, burying himself balls-deep. His arms immediately went beneath her knees, pushing them up close to her head as he continued to thrust into her over and over.

Cathe shut out the world and let herself become one with this giant of a man now owning her body. He was dangerously close to owning her heart too, she admitted as his roar echoed off the walls of the small room. The feel of his warm seed bathing her insides triggered another round of contractions, leaving her in a mindless heap of unimaginable bliss.

Chapter Twelve

Bryne couldn't catch his breath. His heartbeat thumped with a deafening bass, drowning out the sound of his heavy breathing. He lifted his head and gazed down at his beautiful Cathe lying beneath him. "Witch."

"That was the most amazing feeling ever," she breathed, blinking up at him. Her sky-blue eyes were hypnotizing in their allure.

The corner of his mouth lifted. "Even though it was rushed?"

"Rushed?" she repeated in surprise.

He brushed a kiss across her soft lips. "I wanted you too much," he whispered, raking his teeth over her chin. "So much that I skipped over a few things." He nipped at her neck as he slowly slid down her body, dipping inside her navel before coasting over her soft mound. "Such as this delectably enticing peach."

"Bryne..."

His eyes slid closed with the sound of his name falling from her lips, the sweet feel of her hands in his hair as he gently swiped his tongue over her swollen clit.

He growled against her, vibrating her sensitive bundle of nerves only to suck the swollen nub into his mouth and lash it with the tip of his tongue.

The sounds coming from her drove him over the edge, but nothing compared to the scream that ripped from her as she shuddered against his mouth, pulling him closer with her fingers locked in his hair.

Bryne continued to lick her inner thighs with tender strokes until her shivering slowed and eventually stopped. "You taste better than any peach I've ever had."

Cathe's fingers loosened in his hair. "I would return the favor, but I'm not sure I could get my lips around your giant size."

He rose up on his knees and flipped her to her stomach. "It's a curse. What can I say?" Pulling her to a kneeling position in front of him, he gripped his now-hard shaft and aligned it with her opening. "You better hold on."

She gasped as he inched forward, stretching her to accommodate his girth. "Relax; you were made for me, my sweet witch," he murmured, easing her upper body down to the mattress.

The sight of her hands clenching the blankets and her luscious ass in the air had to be the most erotic vision he'd ever seen. It took considerable effort to keep from thrusting hard and deep.

"You belong to me." He entered another inch, gritting his teeth to keep from spilling his seed too fast. "Tell me, my witch. Tell me you are mine," he growled, filling her a little more.

"I can't take you moving so slow. Please, hurry."

"I can hurt you in this position," he protested, feeding her more of his swollen cock until the pressure became too much.

"Oh, God, Bryne. Don't make me beg." She rose up on her arms and pushed back against him.

Bryne locked his hands on her hips and thrust, burying himself as deep as her body would allow, only to pull back and slam into her again. Harder and faster he pistoned into her, fueled by her sexy cries of pleasure.

Her arms suddenly folded, and her pussy clamped down on his cock so tight his seed unexpectedly erupted. He jerked her ass tightly against him as jet after jet of his semen continued to wrench from his body in a mind-shattering orgasm.

Time passed in slow motion while Bryne fought for control. In all the years he'd spent perfecting the art of sex, he'd never been reduced to an inept, clumsy schoolboy in bed before. Until now. "Are you hurt?"

She shook her head but kept her eyes closed.

He gently pulled from her body and turned her over. "Look at me."

Her lids lifted, and what he saw there twisted his gut. "I did hurt you."

"No," she assured him, wiping the tears from her eyes.

"Then why do you cry? What did I do? Tell me so that I can make it better."

"You wouldn't understand."

Bryne stretched out his body on the mattress and pulled her against his side with her head resting on his shoulder. "Try me."

* * * *

"I'm afraid," Cathe admitted, staring up at the water-stained ceiling of Betty's family home.

Adair's arms tightened around her. "Afraid of…?"

"I don't know where to start."

"How about the beginning?"

Cathe took a deep breath and curled up closer to his side. "When I was in college, I fell in love with a guy named Craig Dyson. We met in the parking lot my second week there.

His space happened to be assigned next to mine."

"What is a parking lot?"

"You know how you have horses that take you from one place to another?" She continued at his nod. "Well, we use cars in the twenty-first century."

"Cars?"

"Okay, imagine a buggy that moved without the help of an animal. There would be this big metal thing called an engine that used water and fuel to make it run, and you steer it by holding onto a small wheel."

"Impossible, but we will get back to that later. Tell me about this Craig Dyson." The stiff set of Bryne's shoulders told her he wasn't pleased by her love admission.

"We were together for a couple of years, and I ended up pregnant."

Bryne stilled, but said nothing.

"On February tenth, which was my birthday, Craig called wanting to take me for a ride on a motorcycle I'd bought him a week before. I tried talking him out of it because a storm was coming, and I knew it would be dangerous if we got caught in it."

Bryne shifted next to her. "Go on."

"Nothing I said would sway him from his reckless behavior, so I went, thinking I could somehow make sure he stayed safe."

Cathe took a ragged breath, finding it difficult to talk about the past. "The storm blew in on us less than two blocks from home. Craig lost control of the bike, and we crashed into an oncoming car. He died instantly."

"And the baby?" Bryne's deep voice penetrated her painful memories.

"I miscarried in the hospital later that night. The damage done during the accident was far too extensive, and I...I was left unable to have future children."

She was suddenly flipped to her back with Bryne looming over her. "Do you think I would not want you even if you could not bear me children?"

Tears dripped from the corners of her eyes. "I read in the book that you have a son and a daughter. I don't recall her name, but the boy's I remember because it was the name I had picked out if I would have ever had a son."

"What was it?"

"Isaac. Craig didn't like it. He said it was too biblical."

"You still love him." It wasn't a question.

"Yes. No. I don't know, Bryne. The only thing I can be sure of is the fact that I have never been able to give my heart to another. Not even close."

Bryne stood and gathered up his clothes.

"Where are you going?"

"To bathe and hunt for food. I will collect water from the river so that you can freshen up." He pulled on his pants and snatched up his boots before heading toward the door.

"Wait." Wrapping a blanket around her nude form, Cathe jumped to her feet. "You are the first person I have opened up to since the accident. You're just going to walk out angry?"

The look in his eyes tore at her heart. "It is not anger that you see. I cannot compete with a ghost, Catherine Grier, no matter how strong my feelings are for you." He turned and left without looking back.

* * * *

Bryne had never hated another as much as he did Craig Dyson in that moment. Even dead, the guy still owned Cathe's heart.

He stripped out of his pants and dove into the icy Matanzas River, reveling in the bite of the freezing water on his skin; anything to distract him from the jealousy ripping apart his insides.

Lathering up with the cake of soap he'd grabbed on his way out, Bryne thought of the outlandish story he'd just heard only minutes after losing himself in Cathe's amazing body.

Impossible as it seemed, he wondered if she could be telling the truth. Did she really come from the twenty-first century?

She had talked about strange things he'd never heard of, things that couldn't possibly be real, and yet she had described them in a way that made them believable.

Perhaps she really was a witch, and yet Bryne hadn't sensed an evil bone in her beautiful body. On the contrary, she'd told him the truth when a lie would have served her better—at least what he assumed that she perceived to be the truth.

Bryne finished his bath and trudged his way back to the shore to dry off. He wasn't sure what to believe when it came to Cathe. One thing he was certain of, he was falling in love with her and had no idea how much time he had to convince to stay.

"I'm sorry if I hurt you." Her sweet voice penetrated his numb brain, bringing him out of his musing.

He kept his back to her while he dried the water from his freezing body. "I am trying hard to believe in you, Catherine Grier. My mind screams that you are either crazy or you truly are a witch, but my heart says you speak the truth."

"I am not lying."

He turned to face her. "I understand that you believe what you say to be true, but I need evidence. Prove it to me."

"How am I to do that?"

Bryne finished drying off and picked up his clothes. "Take that stick over there and draw me a picture of this car you spoke of. Explain how it works."

Cathe snatched up the stick and went to work drawing in the sand while Bryne finished pulling on his remaining clothes.

She pointed to a strange-looking contraption she'd created in the dirt. "This is a car, and the one next to it is a truck." She went on to explain everything from the makings of engines to seatbelts, airbags, and tires.

Bryne was floored. Everything she'd told him made sense on some level, even if it seemed impossible. "And the homes?"

"They aren't much different than the homes of your era, other than the fact that they have electricity, which isn't discovered until the late 1700's and later used inside homes in the early 1800's."

Bryne followed Cathe back inside, listening attentively for the next hour as she explained everything from electricity to televisions.

"You understand how hard for me it is to believe all this?" he voiced, pinching the bridge of his nose.

"About as hard as it is for me to comprehend how I woke up nearly two hundred and fifty years in the past, I'm sure."

Somewhere deep inside he knew she spoke the truth, and that unnerved him nearly as much as her leaving him did. "If you are right about all of this, then you plan on returning home some day."

"Yes. I have a career, a life, and my family is there. I have no idea why or how I came to be here, but I can't stay. I was born in a different time. It can't be right that I am here."

The pain that statement caused was soon replaced with anger at her next words.

"I don't understand why I wasn't sent back to the day before the motorcycle accident, so that I could have prevented it. Craig and the baby would both be alive, and I wouldn't be a shell of the woman I was meant to be."

"If you went back and he'd died some other way, would you continue to follow him through time, attempting to save him over and over? What is meant to be will always find a way if it is God's will."

"You think it was God that sent me here?"

"Perhaps."

"What possible reason would he have for doing that? No. It wasn't God that sent me; it was an old crone with a strange-looking book. She is the one I need to find if I am to get home again."

Chapter Thirteen

Words continued to pour from Cathe like a fountain—hurtful, angry words that she couldn't seem to stop. "If this were God's doing, he would give me back what I lost, what I've craved every day of my life since then."

Bryne flinched as if she'd slapped him and turned back toward the door. "I'm going to get dinner." The door slammed shut behind him.

Cathe hated herself in that moment. Bryne couldn't help that she'd landed in his life anymore than he could her erase her past.

She trailed over to the window and watched him stalk off toward the woods. Her stomach fluttered with the memory of him taking her earlier. She'd never been so thoroughly loved before, not even by Craig.

After several minutes of staring at the tree line Adair had disappeared into, Cathe set about adding more wood to the stove.

Setting a pot of water on top to heat, she gathered up her torn dress and plopped down into a wooden chair to study the destruction. Without a needle and thread, she was left with little option but to cut the dress at the waist and fashion a much shorter skirt.

With a little creativeness and a lot of patience, she managed to make a halter top held together in the front by strips of material from the dress. It wasn't the most modest outfit she'd ever worn, but it worked.

Cathe bathed as best she could from the pot of warm water she'd heated on the stove and dragged on her makeshift clothes. Ripping off a piece of cloth from the leftover material, she pulled her hair up into a ponytail before slipping on her shoes, wrapping herself in a blanket and stepping outside.

"Go back inside before you become ill. It's too cold for you to be out here."

Cathe started at the sound of Bryne's voice. She hadn't seen or heard him return. "You scared me." She took a step closer. "What are you doing?"

He stood hunched over at the edge of the trees with his back to her. "Something you need not see. Now stay back."

"There is nothing short of a spider that would scare me," she mumbled, moving to stand next to him. "Would you like some help?"

"This does not upset you?" He nodded toward the skinned rabbit splayed out on a tree stump in front of him.

"I don't relish something having to die to feed me, but I'm pretty damn hungry at the moment. I haven't eaten much since my impossible leap through space." She grinned at his incredulous look.

"You are a strange woman, Catherine Grier."

She loved the way he pronounced her name, his English accent bleeding through his newly learned American one. "I can't change who I am, Bryne."

He slowly straightened and pinned her with a look she could get lost in. "I do not want you to change, Cathe, only to make room for me."

Her heart squeezed. "Can't we just enjoy what time we have together? Look, I may not be able to return home, but I have to try. Please understand that I must try."

Something flickered in his eyes. "If that is truly where your heart lies, then I will help you any way I can."

"Thank you." She moved to hug him, and her blanket slipped from her shoulders to pool at her feet.

"Bloody hell." His eyes darkened with desire as he took in her appearance. "What is that?"

"This?" She waved a hand down her body, indicating her makeshift outfit. "I made it while you were out hunting. The dress was ruined, so I salvaged what little I could."

"Little would be correct."

Cathe laughed. "This is actually modest compared to the way a lot of women dress in the twenty-first century."

Adair looked stunned. "But how are they kept from harm? Even the street girls do not show as much skin."

How indeed, Cathe mused. "They aren't kept from harm. Life is different in the future, Bryne. Rape is steadily on the rise and murder is at an all-time high."

"And this is where you want so much to go back to?"

He had a point, she thought, staring into his gunmetal-gray eyes. The concern she saw there tore at her heart.

Cathe snatched up the blanket and quickly wrapped herself in its remaining warmth. She needed to get away from him before she caved and ended up confessing her feelings for him. "I'll just go stoke the fire in the stove."

"You are afraid," he stated as she stepped around him and advanced back toward the house.

She stopped, but couldn't bring herself to face him. "What is it that you think I'm afraid of?"

"Letting go." His voice deepened. "You fear you could not survive having your heart crushed a second time. Whether by fate or deception, the pain is real, and it hurts just the same."

Tears sprang to her eyes, but she blinked them back. "You think you know—"

"I would lay down my life for you, Catherine." His boots crunched the leaves as he took a step toward her. "I would lie, steal, and kill for you," Another step. "But I would never hurt you." He stopped behind her, enclosing her in his arms. "Believe in me."

The tears she'd tried so hard to hold back spilled over to track down her cheeks. "You could die tomorrow by the king's hand, in a hunting accident, or by a band of thieves lurking in the trees. You live in barbaric times, Bryne, with people that kill without fearing consequences. Don't make promises you can't keep."

"Tell me, Catherine. How can there be a book written about me over two hundred years from now if I am to die before I have even accomplished the things worthy of writing about?"

"I don't know. I told you, I only read a few chapters before I fell asleep."

"I must have been a boring subject," he teased, leaning down to nip her earlobe.

Cathe's lips twitched. "There is nothing boring about you, Lord Lunatic."

"Now I am demented? I am not the one claiming to have traveled through time."

"Point taken," she laughed, stepping out of his arms. "Now bring the rabbit in the house and go wash the stink from your hands while I start dinner." She hurried back inside before he noticed the tears lingering on her cheeks.

* * * *

Bryne stood there for a long moment, staring after Cathe's retreating back until she disappeared inside the house. It had taken everything he had not to spin her around and crush her in his arms.

He'd known that she cried from the sound of her voice, the set of her shoulders. He also knew that she hadn't wanted him to see her tears, so he'd settled for humor in hopes of drying her eyes. "Damn you. Witch."

He finished cleaning the rabbit and trekked back to the house. The sight that greeted him as he stepped over the threshold would forever be burned into his brain. Cathe stood over the stove in her scandalous clothing, leaving virtually nothing to the imagination.

His cock grew instantly hard as she bent forward to adjust the fire. He cleared his throat, alerting her to his presence. "Where would you like for me to put this?"

She indicated a pot on the stovetop. "Ellis packed me some food for a few days. I have some herbs and a few potatoes to go with it."

"I see that you are on a first-name basis with Burland."

"Where I come from, everyone is known by their first name unless it's business related. Then it's common courtesy to use surnames."

The future had strange ways, he surmised, staring at the even stranger woman before him. "How do the men address your women?"

"It may come as a shock to you, but women actually have the same rights as the men, all slaves are freed, and everyone is equal."

"I do not own slaves, and I pay my servants well," he defended. "I have never had a desire to possess another person. Nor do I feel the Spaniards had the right to conquer the Natives and take their lands, or that the king should have taken mine and forced me to live here."

She tilted her head to the side. "But you seem to love St. Augustine."

"Aye. I grew to appreciate its beauty and lack of politics."

"Tell me about the wife and child you lost."

"Maria and I hadn't been married long when she gave birth to our son. She died of diphtheria and the child passed shortly after."

Cathe sat in a chair near the stove. "Did you love her?"

"I…I cared for her," Bryne stated quietly.

"What age was your son when he passed?"

An old, familiar grief took the place of his hunger. He dropped into the chair across from Cathe's. "Barely a month old. He died in my arms, just went to sleep and never woke again. I buried him next to his mother before my castle was burned to the ground."

"I'm so sorry," Cathe whispered, sorrow evident in her voice. She stood and moved to the front of his chair and stood between his knees. "The pain never leaves us, but it does dull over time."

Bryne pulled her onto his lap and crushed her against him. "I feel no sadness when I am with you."

She softly kissed his neck. "I…"

He pulled back to search her face when she didn't finish. "You what?"

"I just had an epiphany." She jumped from his lap to pace in front of his chair. "I was at my bookstore when I first received possession of the book. The old crone that brought it to me disappeared before I could question her about it."

Bryne had a feeling he knew where her thoughts were headed. He didn't have to wait long to confirm his suspicions were correct.

"Maybe the book or the crone is at that same location." She suddenly stopped and blinked at him. "I have to go there. I mean, if my—"

"Whoa. Slow down a minute. You said that you were in Pensacola before you awoke here. It would seem to me that St. Augustine holds all the answers."

"What do you mean?"

"It is where the accident happened that changed your life, and it is also where you were dropped into my bed, into my heart." He rose to his feet also. "Before we go traipsing off to unknown territory, we will search here first."

"But where would we start?"

"We find the place that marked your life. The place of the accident."

"It was on Cordova Street, between Castle de San Marcos and Flagler College where we went to school."

"Castillo de San Marcos is less than half a day's ride from my home. I know not of Flagler College."

"That's because it isn't founded until the mid 1900's…around the time that I was born."

Bryne still found it hard to conceive that Cathe was actually born over two hundred years in the future. "Do you think you can find the location?"

"Yes. I went there enough times that I should be able to recognize a familiar landmark—something that is still standing in the twenty-first century."

"We will return to my home at first light, gather supplies, and head on to Castillo de San Marcos shortly after noon tomorrow."

"Why can't we go straight there?"

He looked her over from head to feet. "You forget what century you are in, my witch. We would never make it there alive with you dressed in that attire." Not that he didn't appreciate her attire or the lack thereof, he mentally concurred, but he refused to allow another man to look upon what belonged to him.

"We'll do it your way then. Mind if I ask you for a favor?"

"You may."

"Can we not spend today dwelling on the bad? I just want to enjoy our time together, to make memories that I can take back with me."

She could have kicked him in the gut and it would not have hurt as much as the thought of her leaving. "As you wish."

"Perfect. You relax while I get lunch started."

Relax while you plot to leave me? Not a chance in Hades.

Chapter Fourteen

Cathe watched Bryne's every move as she cut up potatoes for their stew. The restless set of his shoulders gave away his feelings. He was angry, that much she surmised. And who could blame him? She was feeling some anger of her own.

The bone-deep grievances that life had previously thrown at her should be enough, yet here she was being ripped apart once again. Only this time by her own hand.

Why couldn't Bryne have been born in her time or she born in his? Wasn't it enough that her own heart would ache when she left, but did his have to break also? She kept telling herself that she was meant to return. She could never give him the family that he deserved, and she feared he would grow to resent her for it.

She finished loading the pot with vegetables and spices before covering it with a lid. "It needs to cook for a couple of hours. I hope you're not too hungry."

"I'll live. Would you like to go for a ride along the beach while the stew cooks?"

"Oh, I would love that. Just let me grab a blanket." She briefly touched his hand on her way to the bedroom.

"Take your time. I'll ready the horse," he called as she disappeared into the room.

Sadness settled over her like a cloak with the thought of never seeing him again, but she shook it off. She wrapped herself in a blanket and hurried outside, determined to enjoy what time she had left.

"You grow more beautiful each time I gaze upon you," Bryne announced from his position on the stallion's back.

A blush spread up her neck. "I bet you say that to all the horses."

He grinned, the smile making him even more gorgeous. "Only the mares."

"Just as I thought," she retorted, returning his smile. "We're riding bareback?"

He leaned down with his hands extended toward her. "We are today. Grab on."

"Here, take this." She handed him the blanket before sliding her palms into his and allowing him to pull her up in front of him to straddle the great beast named Reaper. "He's huge."

"I bet you say that to all the horses," he teased from behind her.

"Only the stallions."

With a chuckle he wrapped the blanket around her, enclosed her in his arms, and kicked the giant horse into canter.

It felt amazing being with Adair; the chilly wind in her face, the heat of his body along her back. "Thank you for this. It was a great idea."

Bryne pulled up on the reins, slowing the horse to a stop. The feel of his breath on her neck sent chills across her skin, and not from the weather.

He nuzzled her throat. "I want you."

"Now?" She gasped as he lowered the blanket and halter top down her shoulders.

"Right now." He suddenly lifted her, settling her across his lap. His mouth covered hers in a kiss that left her dizzy with desire.

Somewhere in the far reaches of her mind, Cathe knew she should put a stop to things before they got out of control again, but she couldn't bring herself to do it. She wanted him more than anything she could imagine.

He abruptly broke off the kiss, dragged his mouth down her throat, over her chest, and closed his warm, wet lips around her aching nipple.

Cathe's hands flew to his hair, holding him tight…craving, seeking something that only he could give. "Please."

He didn't answer, only pushed her makeshift skirt up to her hips. Her nipple popped free of his mouth.

"Open for me," he commanded in a low voice. His palm coasted over her knee and along the inside of her thigh.

Cathe could no more stop herself from obeying than she could stop him from slipping his fingers through her slit to the place she craved him most.

Her head fell back in ecstasy as he penetrated her with first one than two of his thick, callused fingers.

His thumb pressed against her clit, sliding in slow, gentle circles. "I want you, Catherine, more than I have ever wanted another."

"Yes." Consequences be damned, she thought, moving her hips in time with his fingers. She craved him just as much.

"Grab onto me," Bryan demanded through clenched teeth.

Cathe wrapped both arms around his neck as he removed his fingers from the juncture of her thighs to free his cock from its confines.

Lifting her, he twisted her to face him until her legs straddled his waist, and he slowly lowered her.

The feeling of his engorged cock pressing against her opening created a need too powerful to resist. "Hurry," she moaned, locking her ankles behind his back.

He thrust, burying himself as deep as their position would allow.

Cathe cried out with the power of his entry. She could only hold onto him as he kicked the stallion into motion, creating an up-and-down movement of their bodies, a natural gravitational pull between horse and man as they became one with nature, with themselves and the beast beneath them.

The drive of his hips pushing his cock deeper inside her, stretching her, caressing her, the chill on her exposed skin, the wind in her hair, the look in his eyes—all collided together to create an orgasm so powerful that she had to bite the inside of her cheek to keep from screaming out.

He suddenly jerked her hard against his body, engulfed her in his arms, and slanted his mouth over hers, leaving her no choice but to swallow his shout as he released his seed deep inside her womb.

Cathe held onto him for long moments while shudders racked his large frame and orgasmic contractions continued to seize her insides, making it difficult to turn him loose.

He loosened his hold on her to tug the horse to a stop. "You are going to be the death of me."

"What a way to go," she muttered against his chest. "How did you keep from dropping the reins?"

"Very carefully." He laughed. "Let's get you straightened out before we are spotted out here. As much as I love touching your creamy-white arse, I would hate to have to kill someone over it."

"Arse? You do realize I'll never let you live that down."

"Does that mean that you plan to stay?"

Pain sliced through her heart at his words. As much as she would love to stick around and see where things went with the handsome earl, she couldn't. "I'm sorry."

* * * *

The continued trip down the beach felt like heaven to Bryne. The woman he loved sat before him, pointing out shells, birds, and several other breathtaking sights that nature had to offer. "Tell me of your life now."

She leaned her head back against his shoulder, leaving the tops of her breasts exposed to his gaze. "I am a retired attorney with many acquaintances and very few friends."

"How come so few?"

"You make a lot of enemies in my line of work."

"I see. What of the bookstore?"

"It's a historical landmark and I couldn't bear to see it torn down, so I bought it and refurbished it."

"And does it bring you the friends you so desire?"

She tilted her head back to peer up at him. "Why would you think I desire them?"

He bent and brushed a kiss across her lips. "I saw you with Betty. You love human interaction."

"Everyone does," she muttered, looking ahead once more. "It doesn't mean that I'm not happy being alone."

"I was content to be alone before you awoke in my bed and wreaked havoc on my life."

She glanced up at him again. "I did no such thing. You brought any havoc that was wreaked on your damn self."

Bryne laughed. He couldn't help it. "I suppose I did create a small amount of drama, but in my defense, I thought you to be a witch."

"A small amount? You slung me in a room with Asshat Ansel, who then locked me in a pillory in my damn robe to freeze to death."

He laid his cheek against the top of her head. "I apologize for my distrust in you, and I am truly sorry about turning you over to Ansel. I should have sent him on his way years ago."

A loud sigh came from his riding companion. "You had no way of knowing that I wasn't a witch. If I'd been in your shoes, I would have thought the same thing."

"You forgive me then?"

"I'll think about forgiving you after I've eaten."

Another chuckle bubbled up. Bryne loved the way she so easily made him laugh. "Then by all means, let's go eat."

Making it back to the house in record time, Bryne tied his horse to a nearby shade tree while Cathe went inside to check on dinner.

He brushed the stallion down with gentle strokes. "You like her too, don't you, boy? How do I make her understand the extent of my love for her?" At the horse's neigh, Bryne continued. "Have you ever seen a more beautiful creature?"

"I bet you say that to all the horses." Her soft voice sounded from behind him.

He must be growing soft; he hadn't heard her approach. "Only the mares."

"Obviously not," she chuckled, stepping up to touch Reaper's nose.

Bryne abruptly bent and grabbed her by the legs, threw her over his shoulder, and jogged toward the house with her laughing the entire way.

"Put me down, you big brute," she gasped through another fit of giggles.

He burst inside, ran to the bedroom, and dropped to his knees on the mattress, lowering her to her back beneath him. He gripped her hands, pinning both arms over her head. "Is my little witch ticklish?" With calculated movements, he dipped his chin to her ribcage and dug in.

The ear-piercing squeal and attempt at bucking him off affirmed his suspicions. "I now have all the blackmail I need to keep you quiet about the stallion-mare mix-up."

"Yes. Yes, I promise. Just please stay away from my funny bones," she demanded through another bout of laughter.

"Deal. Let's eat." Jumping to his feet, he pulled her up and swatted her on the butt. "Me, you, stew, now go."

She grinned on her way to the door. "Yes, my big, dumb caveman."

"Dumb?" He chased her into the front room and around the stove a few times before catching her and dragging her kicking and screaming back to the mattress for round two of tickle torture.

They spent the rest of the day and night eating rabbit stew and making love. Bryne had never been as happy as he was in that moment. Titles and lands he could give up. None of it was worth anything to him without Catherine, his witch…his eternal love.

Chapter Fifteen

The next morning went by in a blur of packing and tension. Bryne hadn't said much since they'd made love and bathed in bowls of heated river water. The best day of Cathe's life was about to come to an end, leaving her forever altered.

She glanced back at the rundown house where she'd lost her heart to the legendary Bryne Adair. "I'll miss this place."

"As will I."

Her heart hurt so bad she found it hard to breathe. "If it were meant for me to stay, you would not have fathered the two children the future will later read about."

He pulled her back against him and spurred the horse forward. "Aye. But the past has since been altered by you being here. The children may not be in the book today. And how can you be sure of not bearing offspring since you have traveled back before the accident happened to begin with?"

"I had already thought of that. I went back over two hundred years, it's true, but I arrived here on February tenth, and the accident happened on February sixth. I'm assuming I am the age of twenty three since the surgery scar remains."

"So the crone sent you back this far in time only to leave you barren? It makes no sense."

"None of this does," she replied, blinking to prevent the tears from rising.

"I will take you to the place it all began. If the crone is there and you can return home, I will not stop you. But know this, my sweet Catherine Grier, I will love you beyond the boundaries of time, and no matter how long it takes, I will find you again."

The tears she'd tried so hard to hold back, spilled forth unbidden. "The memory of me may disappear after I'm gone."

"I can only pray that God would not be so cruel."

"And I can only pray that he is." She couldn't bear to imagine him heartbroken and in pain.

Neither of them spoke again as Bryne kicked the horse into a run, not slowing until he crossed the bridge leading to his castle, his home — the one place that she didn't belong.

"My Lord," the servants chorused, running out to greet their master.

Bryne dismounted, and Cathe slid off the stallion's back into Bryne's waiting arms, making sure to keep the blanket tightly wrapped around her.

The sight of Ansel swinging from a noose turned her stomach. She shuddered and rushed toward the castle. "I'm going inside."

"Are you ill?" Bryne called out as she made her way up the wide steps that led to the doors.

"I just need to freshen up before we head out again," she responded over her shoulder.

Betty was waiting for Cathe when she stepped over the threshold. The maid burst forward and encircled Cathe in her arms. "Oh, Miss. I was worried sick about ya. I ain't seen Ellis yet to ask about your welfare. And then Virgil said Lord Adair was goin' after ya. I been ill ever since."

Cathe hugged her back. "I'm fine, really." She let go to step around the maid, quickly closing the blanket. "Lord Adair and I have to leave again within the hour. Is there any way I could talk you into having a bath prepared? I fear I stink after bathing in a freezing river and being forced to take a whore's bath the rest of the time."

"What's a whore's bath, Miss?"

Cathe laughed. She'd temporarily forgotten what century she was in. "Oh, nothing. It's a joke I heard once." She sent Betty a reassuring smile. "I just need a bath."

Betty jumped to do her bidding. "Yes, Miss. I'll see to it right now. Go on up, and I'll take care of everything."

Cathe thanked the maid and took the stairs a little faster than she normally would have. Odd how fears can ease and life can change in so short a time, she thought, stepping off onto the top landing that led to Adair's bedroom.

* * * *

"Word arrived this morning of the king's departure, my Lord," Virgil announced, falling in step next to Adair. "It would seem that his wife is with child and is not doing well."

"He has returned to England?"

"Aye, and not a moment too soon, if you ask me. Let us hope we have a longer reprieve this time. One can only pray that she carries the offspring to term and gives him another shortly after."

Bryne's lips twitched. "That's treasonous talk, Haskell. I would hate to awake in the morning to find you swinging in the breeze next to Ansel over there."

"Speaking of Ansel... Shall I have him taken down? The buzzards are starting to pick at him. I fear I will draw a drink from the well one day and discover an eye floating in the pail, my Lord."

Adair absently nodded, his mind already somewhere else. "Aye. Have him removed. If he has family nearby, they may pick up his remains."

"If there is no one?"

"Then he is to be dumped far from the castle walls. I do not want his stench seeping in to remind me of his filthy paws on my Catherine."

Virgil nodded. "You have Walt readying Reaper again. I am certain he is weary from his exertive run this morning. Perhaps you would take one of the other stallions in his stead?"

"Nay. It wasn't that far. Besides, he will have time to rest while we prepare for our departure. I am not sure what awaits us there, old friend. I trust no other horse but Reaper."

"I understand," Haskell admitted, clasping his hands behind his back. "I can be saddled up and ready to ride in minutes, my Lord."

Bryne knew he couldn't take Virgil with him on his journey to find the book. He had no idea what he and Cathe would find there, if anything at all. The risks were just too high. "With the king gone, I have nothing to watch for but thieves, old friend. You are needed here more than with me."

"As you wish, Sire." Virgil stopped as Bryne made his way up the castle steps.

Adair opened the doors and glanced back at his second-in-command. "You're a good friend, Haskell."

"I try, old man." Virgil grinned and strode off toward the stables.

Once inside, Bryne took the stairs two at a time in a hurry to be with his beautiful witch. Five minutes away from her felt like an eternity.

He rushed into his room to find her seated in a bath, her head lying back against the rim, her eyes closed, and her lips slightly parted. She'd fallen asleep in the tub.

Bryne closed the door and stripped out of his clothes as quietly as he could. He moved around behind her, stepped over the side, and lifted her onto his lap, her back to his front.

"Mmmm, you made it," she murmured without opening her eyes.

He kissed her neck and picked up a cake of strawberry-smelling soap. "You do realize that bees are going to chase us all the way to Castillo de San Marcos," he pointed out while lathering her arms and shoulders.

"That's orange blossom you're thinking of, not strawberries."

"I see. Then fruit flies will swarm us. Either way, insects will definitely smell us coming for miles."

She tilted her face to the side where he could see her sky-blue eyes. "Are you worried about what we will find when we get there?"

"I would be lying if I said no. I am worried about keeping you fed, I worry about keeping you safe, but nothing scares me more than never seeing you again."

"Bryne…"

"Are you certain you wish to leave?"

"No, but I am sure that I need answers. I have to find that crone. She is the only one that can set things right." Cathe turned to face him, straddling his lap. "Suppose I stay and we are happier than we ever imagined, then one day the crone returns to take me back. I couldn't take that."

"That is a chance we will—"

"I cannot give you children, Bryne. That means the two you have are not from me. Don't you see? I am not supposed to be here."

The pain in her eyes tore him apart inside. "To hell with what is meant to be. I could never love another as deeply as I love you."

She cupped the sides of his face and closed her lips over his. Bryne kissed her back with everything he had. All the love he held inside poured from him in that one earth-shattering kiss.

Lifting up on her knees, Cathe aligned herself with his now-throbbing erection and slowly lowered herself onto him. She continued to make love to his mouth as her incredible body fully became one with his.

Bryne forgot to breathe the longer she rode him. Pure ecstasy overtook him, stealing his need to control, to dominate. His head fell back in surrender as an overwhelming emotion burned him alive, forcing everything he'd ever believed in to submit.

Years of bitterness fell away in that moment—the hatred toward his father, the anger at his king—all of it gone in a heartbeat to be replaced with the love of the woman in his arms.

Her soft cries penetrated his passion-induced brain, triggering an orgasm so intense the room shifted before his eyes. Fire raced up his spine, and his entire body locked up with the power of his release.

A distant shout reverberated throughout the room, and it took a moment for Bryne to realize it came from him. He wasn't sure how long he sat there shuddering in her arms before he was able to lift his head.

She stared back at him with a look of wonder in her eyes. "Making love with you is very emotional, Bryne. I feel so deeply connected to you on every level."

He brushed his fingertips down her cheeks. "That is because you are my soul mate."

"I would like to believe that." She reached down and touched the small scar on her abdomen. "But this tells me otherwise."

"That means nothing," he argued, glancing at the smooth white line she'd indicated.

She suddenly stood. "It's getting late."

Bryne rose to his feet also, wrapping his hand around her wrist. "Why must you do this?"

"Do what?"

"Shut me out every time I open myself up to you."

She yanked her wrist free. "Because I'm scared, damn it. Is that what you wanted to hear? I'm afraid of my feelings for you, I'm afraid of losing you, but mostly I'm afraid if I stay here, I'll destroy you."

"You could never destroy me, Catherine. I would give up everything for you— children, titles, lands—all of it to live in that rundown house on the beach with you."

"I know you would, Bryne, and I cannot let that happen."

Chapter Sixteen

The look on Adair's handsome face when he'd stepped out of the tub earlier that day would haunt Cathe for the rest of her life. She hated like hell to hurt him, but the alternative would have been beyond cruel.

She glanced over at him sitting atop Reaper's back, staring straight ahead. "You're not speaking to me now?"

He didn't look at her. "There is nothing left to say."

"I wish I could believe that if I stayed, everything would be okay, Bryne. I really do."

He finally met her gaze. "If it had been Craig's bed you'd awoken in, would you have stayed?"

"That's not fair. We have a history, we—"

"Save it. I have heard enough." He lifted his hand and pointed to something up ahead. "Castillo de San Marcos is through those trees there. Do you see anything you recognize?"

Cathe scanned the area for signs of old landmarks that seemed familiar to her. "I need to see the castle entrance to get a close approximation of how far it is from where the college now sits."

He nodded. "Stay close behind me in case we run into trouble."

Cathe gave her mare lead to follow Reaper, staying far enough back not to crowd the giant stallion as he wound his way through the overgrown foliage.

"I don't see..." Her voice trailed off in wonder as the massive walls of the castle came into view.

"Wow, it's even more magical in its past form. So many changes have been made in the future. Can we go inside?" she asked, entirely too loud.

"Not unless we want to explain our presence here. Perhaps we will come back later if we do not find what you seek." He shifted in his saddle. "The entrance is there. Where do we go from here?"

"That way." She turned her horse toward the south. "Two blocks straight ahead will be where Flagler College will be someday. There is a giant boulder sitting near the grounds that's said to be over three hundred years old, which means it's here now."

The two of them continued on in silence, both searching for the place that had altered Cathe's life over two hundred years in the future.

"There," she pointed out, spurring her horse into a gallop. The giant boulder could be seen in the distance, rising up from the ground in the shape of a head.

Cathe slowed her horse to a stop approximately fifty feet from it and dismounted. She glanced back at the castle before tethering her mare to a low-lying branch and walking south.

Bryne climbed down from his stallion and walked along beside her. "Is this the place?"

"Yes. Just ahead."

"I see nothing," he remarked but continued forward.

Cathe's heart pounded out of control as she came to a stop where Craig and their unborn child were taken from her. "This is it."

She held out her arms and turned in a circle, but nothing magical happened, no hole opened up to swallow her, and no sign of the book. "We were wrong."

"I am sorry there was no sign of the book ," he stated quietly, coming to stand next to her. "If your desire lies in returning home, I will continue to help you search. You happiness is everything to me."

What was she doing? This man, this amazingly handsome and strong man loved her enough to let her go regardless of the pain it would bring to him. She had never witnessed a more selfless act. "Bryne? I love—"

"Why have you come here?"

Cathe sucked in a stunned breath and turned toward the sound of the voice. There, standing next to the boulder stood the old crone from the bookstore.

"I was looking for you." Cathe stumbled forward on shaky legs. "I need your help."

The crone shifted her gaze to Adair. "Seems you have all the help you need."

"You did this to me. To us!" Cathe cried, throwing her hand out in Bryne's direction.

The crone pinned her with an unreadable look. "You do not love him?"

"Don't you see? It doesn't matter how I feel about him. You sent me back a week too late. His life will be ruined if I stay here."

"Your decision would be different had you arrived days before?"

"Yes. I don't know. Why here? Why not the day before the accident in the correct century?"

"You think you would be happy had that accident never happened?" The crone reached out and grasped Cathe's hand. "Very well."

Heat suddenly raced through Cathe's body like fire. Bryne's shout could be heard over her own screams as the surrounding area begin to spin around them faster and faster, constantly changing until her world turned dark.

****

Bryne's legs gave out and his knees buckled beneath him. A lone tear dripped from the corner of his eye as he stared at the place where the love of his life once stood. "No," he groaned, fighting the urge to vomit. "Please, no."

He threw his head back and released a wail he felt wrench from his very soul. He couldn't wrap his mind around what had just happened. She was gone. His beautiful witch had left him before he had a chance to say goodbye.

For the first time in his life, Bryne understood why his father did what he had done. How was he himself supposed to exist in this life without her?

Catherine had told him he would have two children and that he would call his son Isaac, the name she'd always wanted for her own child someday. But she was wrong. He would never have any children that were not with her.

Bryne stayed there for the rest of the day, waiting for her to reappear before he staggered to his feet and climbed onto Reaper's back. Leading the stallion over to Cathe's mare, he gathered her reins and headed in the direction of home.

The trip home was a blur to Bryne as thoughts of the beautiful blonde that had turned his world upside down wreaked havoc on his mind. He saw her everywhere—in the trees, bathing in the water, straddling him on the front of his stallion. "Damn you, witch."

"Where is the lady, my Lord?"

Bryne hadn't realized he'd crossed the bridge and now sat in the center of his courtyard. "She's gone, Walt. See to the horses?" He dismounted and handed the servant the reins.

"Of course, Sire."

With a stiff nod and a quiet thank-you, Bryne meandered toward the castle doors, ignoring the many pleasantries being sent his way.

He stumbled through the door and up the stairs, passing Cathe's favorite maid in the hallway. "See to it that I am not disturbed, Betty. For anything."

"Yes, my Lord. Will the Miss be joinin' ya, Sire?"

The hole in his heart deepened. "No, Betty. She's gone, and she won't be coming back."

"Are ya sure, my Lord? She seemed so taken with ya. I—"

"I am sure, Betty. I want no mention of her name in this castle again," he ground out, entering his room and closing the door behind him.

Thankful the tub had been removed and his bed sheets had been changed, Bryne moved to the window overlooking the courtyard. His gaze strayed to the pillory where Cathe had once been locked, then to the well where her unconscious body had been found.

Grief slammed into him hard enough he had to grip the windowsill to stay standing. She'd known nothing but pain and misery in the short time that she'd been with him—from being accused of witchery to hiding from a vengeful king, he thought in disgust. And Bryne was to blame for it all.

* * * *

Cathe cracked her eyes open and squinted against the afternoon sun. A moan slipped past her lips as she turned her head and took in her surroundings. Dozens of people rushed past in a hurry to reach their cars.

Cars? She sat up so fast her head spun. "Where am I?"

"Where it all began."

Cathe shifted her gaze toward the old crone sitting nearby, leaning against a vehicle. "You took me home."

"In a sense."

She glanced around, taking in the different cars and trucks littering the parking lot before turning back to the crone. "That's my car you're leaning against. I sold it to buy Craig that motorcycle."

"I can't make it this afternoon," a nearby voice was saying. "Cathe and I are going to the game."

"Craig?" Cathe jumped to her feet in time to watch her old flame dig out his keys and grin at the guy now leaning against the hood of his car.

"He can't hear you," the crone murmured.

"What? Why not?"

The old woman slowly got to her feet. "This is Craig's life a year before the motorcycle accident."

Cathe's stomach tightened. "Before we became pregnant."

"Do you love him?"

"I loved him very much," Cathe whispered, staring at the man she spent years pining over.

"It better be me you're talking about," Craig teased, taking a step toward her. "Where did you come from?"

"You can see me?" Cathe took a hesitant step forward.

"Have you been drinking already?" He grinned and threw his arm around her shoulder, pulling her tightly against his body. "Were you sitting out here in your car all this time? It's hot as hell out here."

Cathe couldn't take her gaze from his face. She'd shed enough tears to create an ocean after his death, dreamed a thousand dreams where he'd ridden off into the sunset with her by his side...so why was it Bryne's face she craved to see in this moment?

Her heart began to pound and her palms grew sweaty. "Yes, I...I was in my car."

"Is something wrong, sweetheart?" Craig removed his arms and turned her toward him, his gaze searching her face.

Bryne's intense gray eyes flashed through her mind, his laughter, his touch, his unconditional love. She took Craig's hand in hers. "You're a special man, Craig Dyson, and I have no doubt that you will make some woman a wonderful husband someday, but that woman isn't me."

He squeezed her fingers. "What are you saying?"

"I'm so sorry for hurting you, but you deserve nothing less than complete honesty." She took a deep breath and met his gaze. "I'm in love with someone else."

"You cheated on me?" He moved back a few feet, gaping at her.

"No. I never cheated on you." And she didn't. She hadn't met Bryne until nearly thirty years after the motorcycle accident.

"Then what the hell is all this? When did you meet him, Cathe? You and I have been together for a damn year."

Cathe didn't know what to say to that. "You will realize someday that I wasn't the one for you. I can only hope that you will remember me with fondness as I will you." She quickly closed the distance between them, stood on her tiptoes, and softly kissed his cheek. "Goodbye, Craig."

Before he could stop her, she turned away and made her way back to her car where the crone waited.

"Why did you bring me here? He could have gone on with his life without me hurting him like that."

"History would have repeated itself otherwise," the old woman responded, matter of fact.

"What happens now?"

"Where does your heart lead you?"

"You know where my heart lies!" Cathe cried. "But his life would be ruined with me. I can't give him children; his king thinks I'm a witch. The risks associated with me are far too high."

"Do you not think that is his decision to make?"

"But in the book, he has a daughter and a son named Isaac. How am—"

The crone suddenly laid her palm against Cathe's abdomen. "The tie has been severed with Dyson. There was no accident."

Tears sprang to Cathe's eyes. "You mean I'm not barren?"

The old woman nodded and turned to go. "Live a long and happy life, Catherine Grier."

"Wait!" Cathe called out with more than a little desperation. "How do I get back to Bryne?"

The wind began to swirl as the crone stopped and faced her. "Do you love him enough to give up your existence for him? Once you cross over, your life here is no more. You can never return."

"I would die for him," Cathe affirmed, stumbling forward against the growing wind.

"Very well." The old woman in the tattered clothes began to fade before Cathe's eyes and the most beautiful voice she'd ever heard, echoed inside her mind. *"Escape the bonds of the mortal mind, imprisoned no more by the realms of time..."*

* * * *

The morning sun had just peaked over the horizon as Bryne made his way toward the stables. Perhaps a ride would do him good, he thought with a jaw-popping yawn. He hadn't slept much since Cathe's departure. A vision of her beautiful face appeared every time he closed his eyes.

"Where might you be going at this hour, my Lord?"

Bryne eyed his second-in-command. "I should ask you the same question."

"Ah. Avoidance. How very clever of you. It will not deter me in the least."

"You're insufferable, Virgil. If you must know, I am going for a ride along the beach. I need the fresh air and a change of scenery."

Haskell laid his hand on Bryne's arm. "You have to let her go, old man, before you drive yourself mad."

"I am already there, my friend."

"You will find another—"

"No. I had my happiness, Virgil. As short-lived as it was…"

Haskell nodded and stepped back. "You know where to find me, Sire."

"Aye. I do," Bryne agreed quietly before resuming his journey to the stables.

The smell of hay greeted Bryne as he stepped inside and pulled the door shut. He could barely see without the help of a lamp, but he didn't care. He'd walked to his stallion's stall enough times; he could get there blindfolded.

"Hey there," Bryne crooned before opening the stall door and stepping inside. Reaper neighed, bumping Adair's hand with his head.

"It's good to see you too, boy." He gently rubbed the giant stallion's nose. "Feel up to a ride this morning?"

Another neigh along with a head toss told Bryne the horse was probably raring to go as much as he was.

Adair coasted his palm down the side of Reaper's neck and glanced at the Arabian barely visible in the next stall. "You like her, don't you?" he asked while continuing to caress his horse's mane. "She's a pretty one, but not as handsome as you, ole boy."

"I bet you say that to all the horses."

Bryne stilled, afraid his mind had finally snapped. "Only the mares," he whispered, unwilling to believe it could really be her.

He slowly turned, peering into the darkness. "Catherine?"

She stepped from the shadows, pale and even more beautiful than he remembered. "Bryne…"

Adair staggered forward, sinking to his knees in front of her. He buried his face against her stomach and wrapped his arms around her hips. "Are you really here, my witch? Or has my mind finally left me?"

She dropped to her knees and cupped his face, bringing his gaze up to hers. "I'm here, my Lord Adair, and I vow to you that I'll never leave you again."

He crushed her against him, burying his face in her hair. "I cannot live without you, Catherine, offspring or no; titles and lands be damned."

Cathe pulled back and brushed his lips with hers. "You don't have to give up anything for me, Bryne. The children in the book are ours. I just didn't read far enough ahead to know that."

He brought his hand down to cover her stomach. "You are not barren then?"

"Nay," she replied in his native language. "I am not barren."

"Catherine Grier, witch of my heart, will you be my bride?"

"Aye, Lord Adair, I would be most honored."

Epilogue

Five Years Later

"Faster, Papa!" Isaac cried from his position on Reaper's back.

Adair laughed, adjusting the boy higher up on his lap. "We have left your mother too far behind." He pulled up on the reins, giving her time to catch up.

"Mama is slow," the child announced in his soft child's voice.

"That's because Mama carries your little sister in her belly. She can't move as quickly as we can."

Cathe stopped her horse next to them. "This looks like a good place to fish to me."

Bryne dismounted, lifting Isaac down with him before rushing to help his beautiful wife to the ground. He grinned watching her waddle to the water's edge.

"Where are the poles?" she asked, easing down to the sand to remove her shoes.

"There." Bryne pointed to a copse of bushes at the top of the hill.

"I'll get it, Papa," Isaac proclaimed, taking off in a full run.

Adair shook his head, watching his son fall several times before reaching the tree line. "He is as clumsy as his mother." He grinned and knelt at her feet. "Allow me."

Isaac returned carrying three fishing poles and a basket by the time Bryne finished removing his wife's shoes. "Thank you, son. Set it right there and help me spread the blanket."

"When did you do all this?" Cathe asked, indicating the surprise picnic.

"I had Betty prepare it while you were taking your bath," Bryne admitted, standing to unfold the blanket.

Cathe smiled, a beautiful smile that would always hold the power to turn him to mush. "You never cease to amaze me, husband. Thank you for being you."

He reached down and pulled her to her feet. "No regrets, my witch?"

"Maybe just one," she murmured, lowering her eyes.

His stomach tightened with dread. "Tell me."

"That I didn't make love to you this morning."

Relief poured through him with her admission. "I should turn you over my knee for that."

She grinned up at him. "That's what I was hoping for."

"Insatiable wench."

"You created this monster, Lord Adair. Now you must deal with it."

He bent and kissed her lips. "And deal with it, I shall...the second we arrive home."

"Promises, promises." She brushed his hair back from his face. "I love you, Bryne Adair."

"And I love you, Catherine Adair."

"Any word from the king?"

"How did you know that George was here? I only found out last night."

"I shan't divulge my sources," she stated with a twinkle in her eyes.

Bryne sighed and wrapped her in his arms. "According to his letter, he has come in hopes of persuading us to accept his gift of rebuilding my castle and giving back my lands along with the gold my father left me."

"And what does he want in exchange?"

"Your service to the crown."

She took a step back, a frown on her beautiful face. "What kind of service?"

"He still believes you to be a witch. It is my opinion that he's a little afraid of you."

"Do you really want to go back to England? I will do what you want, Bryne. I'm happy wherever you are."

"Nay, my beautiful temptress, I prefer to remain here with you, spending the rest of my days making you happy."

"What about me, Papa?" Isaac clutched at Bryne's leg, staring up at him with trusting eyes.

"Absolutely, my son." He lifted the child's chubby little body into his arms and turned to face the water. "You see? We are writing our own story from here on out."

Cathe stepped up beside him and snuggled against his side. "What happens next, my Lord?"

He shrugged his shoulders, staring out at the crashing waves. "Turn the page…"

Worlds Apart

Turn the Page Series

Book Two

Phoebe Dockery had screwed up this time. Sweat trickled down her back as she raced through the back alleys of Bourbon Street, staying one step ahead of New Orleans' finest.

She'd known better than to pull the trigger, but fear and torture were powerful motivators. She couldn't bear the pain again, the hurt, the suffering, the feel of his disgusting touch.

"Go on, girl, before you bring the cops down here looking for you. I don't need the trouble."

Phoebe drew her Beretta and squinted into the darkness. "Stay where you are, or I'll shoot."

"What did you do to warrant the entire police force casing the streets for you?"

"That's none of your business," she barked, pressing deeper into the shadows as the spotlight from a patrol car sliced through the alley.

"I can help you."

"And why should I trust you?"

A figure suddenly stepped forward, and Phoebe's breath caught. A frail old woman wearing a long tattered coat and a knitted cap stared back at her.

"You do not have to trust me, girl. You only have to come with me if you want to live."

Phoebe slowly got to her feet. "Who are you?"

"It does not matter who I am. It only matters who you are and that you are not meant to die on this day."

"What makes you think I'm going to die?"

The old woman drew closer, until she stood in the center of the alley. The moonlight reflected off her glasses, making it impossible to see her eyes. "Your life ends tonight on this backstreet, Phoebe Dockery. Unless you come with me."

"How do you know my name?" Phoebe hissed, ducking a stray spotlight once again.

"It matters not. Now hurry. We must make haste." The old woman turned back the way she'd come.

With her heart hammering in her ears, Phoebe lurched forward. "Wait up," she called, rushing to catch up.

"In here." The old woman opened a door to a rundown apartment building and ushered Phoebe inside.

"Who lives here?" Phoebe asked, following her rescuer up a flight of stairs to the second-floor landing.

"I do." The crone unlocked the door and threw it wide. "Hurry before you are seen."

With one more look back to assure herself that she wasn't followed, Phoebe stepped over the threshold.

As far as furnishings went, the woman barely had any, but the place appeared clean, and other than a slight moldy smell it didn't stink.

Phoebe rushed to the window and pulled the curtain back far enough to have a clear view of the streets below. Keeping her gaze trained on the officers on foot, she asked, "How do you know my name?"

"You are all over the news. Armed and dangerous. The cops have been ordered to shoot you on sight."

Nausea rolled through Phoebe's gut, but she swallowed it back. "Then why are you helping me?"

"Someone helped me once when I needed it. Besides, if my stepfather had done to me what yours has been doing to you all these years, I would have killed him too."

The breath whooshed from Phoebe so fast she felt faint. She spun to face the old crone. "How did you—"

"You'll be safe here tonight. Tomorrow, you will go far from this place and never look back." She tossed a blanket onto the small couch. "Get some sleep, child." She opened a door a few feet away and disappeared inside.

Pulling the curtain closed, Phoebe crawled onto the well-worn couch and dragged the thin blanket up to her neck.

The night's events played through her mind like a mantra, leaving her mentally exhausted. She would never have killed Ricardo had he not pulled a knife on her when she'd tried to leave. She'd shot him in a fit of panic.

He'd been molesting her for years. The police had never been any help to her. Hell, her own mother didn't believe her. Why would the cops be any different?

Phoebe sat up and studied the room. A large picture of fruit rested above a small dining table that sat near the kitchen with a large book resting on top.

Realizing that sleep wasn't an option, she threw back the blanket trailed and over to the table to check out the title. *Turn the Page. How clever.*

She gingerly lifted the book and took it back to the couch in hopes of reading herself into oblivion. Stories had always been her escape from Ricardo.

The snake on the front felt cold to the touch as she lightly ran her fingers over it before opening the cover to the first page. A faded library card rested in a sleeve that had seen better days, and she pulled it free to scan the list of names. The last name on the list was dated one year before. *Well, Catherine Grier, let's see what struck your fancy…*

Coming soon!

Titles by Ditter Kellen

The Seeker Series

Ember Burns

Ember Learns
Ember Yearns
Ember Discerns
Ember Turns
Five Book Box Set available

Scruples Series

SCRUPLES

Secret Series

Lydia's Secret

Turn the Page Series

Turn the page- Book One

Worlds Apart-Book Two – Coming Soon!

Co-written with Dawn Montgomery

Thunder and Roses

pg. 194

FoxFire
Haunting Melody St. Claire

DITTER KELLEN

A former 911 dispatcher turned author, Ditter Kellen has been in love with romance for over twenty years. To say she's addicted to reading is an understatement. Her eBook reader is an extension of her and holds many of her fantasies and secrets. It's filled with dragons, shifters, vampires, ghosts and many more jaw-dropping characters who keep her entertained on a daily basis. Ditter's love of paranormal and outrageous imagination have conspired together to bring her where she is today...sitting in front of her computer allowing them free rein. Writing is her passion, what she was born to do. I hope you will enjoy reading her stories as much as she loves spinning them. Ditter resides in Florida with her husband and many unique farm animals. She adores French fries and her phone is permanently attached to her ear. You can contact Ditter by email: ditterthegreat@hotmail.com